碧廬

THE TURN OF THE SCREW

冤孽

原著 _ Henry James

改寫 _ Jennifer Gascoigne

譯者 _ 盧相如

ABOUT THIS BOOK

For the Student

🎧 Listen to the story and do some activities on your Audio CD.

🗩 Talk about the story.

⭐ Prepare for Cambridge English: Preliminary (PET) for schools.

For the Teacher

 A state-of-the-art interactive learning environment with 1000s of free online self-correcting activities for your chosen readers.

Go to our Readers Resource site for information on using readers and downloadable Resource Sheets, photocopiable Worksheets, and Tapescripts. www.helblingreaders.com

For lots of great ideas on using Graded Readers consult Reading Matters, the Teacher's Guide to using Helbling Readers.

Level 4 Structures

Sequencing of future tenses	Could / was able to / managed to
Present perfect plus yet, already, just	Had to / didn't have to
First conditional	Shall / could for offers
Present and past passive	May / can / could for permission
	Might for future possibility
How long?	Make and let
Very / really / quite	Causative have
	Want / ask / tell someone to do something

Structures from lower levels are also included.

CONTENTS

Henry James was born in New York in 1843. He was the second of five children. His parents were wealthy[1] and cultured[2] people. When he was a teenager, the family spent several years traveling around Europe. During this time Henry attended private schools and also studied with private teachers. He learnt to speak several languages and read many books by famous European writers.

At the age of 19 he started studying law at Harvard University. However, he didn't finish the course because he much preferred reading and writing stories to studying law. His first short story was published in 1864. After that he decided to devote[3] himself completely to writing.

In 1875 he left America and went to live in France. The following year he moved to England, where he spent the rest of his life. Henry James never married, but he had many friends and a busy social life. In 1915 at the start of World War I he became a British citizen. He died in London in February of the following year.

During his life Henry James wrote over twenty novels. The most well-known[4] include *The Portrait of a Lady* (1881), *The Bostonians* (1886), *The Ambassadors* (1903) and *The Golden Bowl* (1904). These novels are now popular films. He also wrote many short stories[5] and novellas[6] (longer than short stories but shorter than novels), plays[7] for the theater, articles[8] for magazines and books about his travels.

1 wealthy [ˈwɛlθɪ] (a.) 富有的
2 cultured [ˈkʌltʃəd] (a.) 有教養的
3 devote [dɪˈvot] (v.) 奉獻
4 well-known [ˈwɛlˈnon] (a.) 眾所周知的
5 short story 短篇小說
6 novella [noˈvɛlə] (n.) 中篇小說
7 play [ple] (n.) 戲劇；劇本
8 article [ˈɑrtɪkl̩] (n.) 文章

ABOUT THE BOOK

Published in 1898, *The Turn of the Screw* is Henry James's best-known[1] ghost story. Ghost stories were very popular at the end of the 19th century, when there was also much interest in the supernatural[2].

James begins his novella with a prologue[3], an introduction to the main story. A group of friends is spending Christmas together in an old country house. One evening they decide to tell each other ghost stories. One of the guests says that he once read a very frightening one. Of course everyone wants to hear it, so he has the pages of the story sent from his house in London. A couple of nights later he reads it to his friends.

1 best-known [`bɛst`non] (a.) 最有名的
2 supernatural [ˌsupə`nætʃərəl]
   (a.) 超自然的 (n.) 超自然力量
3 prologue [`pro͵lɔg] (n.) 序言；前言
4 governess [`gʌvənɪs] (n.) 女家庭教師
5 employ [ɪm`plɔɪ] (v.) 雇用
6 evil [`ivl] (a.) 邪惡的
7 convinced [kən`vɪnst] (a.) 確信的
8 pupil [`pjupl] (n.) 小學生；學生

The story forms the main part of the novella. It is written by a young governess[4] about her first job.

She is employed[5] by a young, handsome man to look after his young nephew and niece—Miles aged 10 and Flora aged 8. They live in a large house in the country called Bly and they are both very beautiful and good. Soon after her arrival the governess sees—or imagines she sees—the evil[6] ghosts of two dead servants, a man called Quint and a woman called Miss Jessel. She is convinced[7] that the ghosts are communicating with the children and that they are going to hurt them. She decides that she must save her pupils[8] before it is too late.

Are the children really in danger? Or is the governess mad? Henry James leaves it to the reader to decide.

1 Look at the pictures of some of the characters in the story. Which of the words or phrases below describe these characters? Use your dictionary to check the meanings of the words if necessary.

1. 20 years old
2. long, pale face
3. golden curls
4. dressed in black
5. 10 years old
6. red hair

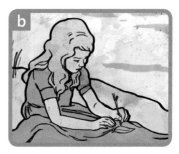

2 Write a short description of each of the characters in Exercise **1**. With a partner read and guess the character.

3 Listen to an extract from the story, when the governess describes her two young pupils, Miles and Flora. Answer the questions below. Put a tick (√) in the correct box.

T F (a) Miles learnt many things by himself.

T F (b) Miles and Flora often had arguments.

4 Match the people with something they do as part of their job.

1. governess
2. headmaster
3. housekeeper
4. maid

_____ a. informs parents about their children's progress

_____ b. teaches children to read and write

_____ c. clears the table after dinner

_____ d. tells servants what to do

5 Complete the extracts from the story with an appropriate word from Exercise **4**.

a. Then I remembered Mrs. Grose's words when the _____'s letter arrived: "All boys are bad sometimes."

b. A _____ let her in and asked her to wait in a small room.

c. The _____ and a little girl appeared at the door to welcome me.

d. Needing to work, she decided to answer an advertisement in a newspaper for the position of _____.

6 Who are the people on pages **55** and **68**? What do you think these women are like? Discuss your ideas with a partner.

7 Match the underlined words in the sentences with the pictures.

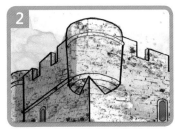

——— (a) Flora and Miles walked up and down the lawn while the governess and the housekeeper talked.

——— (b) The lake at Bly was surrounded by tall reeds.

——— (c) One night the governess saw a woman sitting at the bottom of the staircase.

——— (d) Many of the rooms in the tower were empty.

🔊 **8** The ghosts in the story appear to the governess in different places. Guess three from the list below. Put a tick (√) in the box next to the places. Explain your choices to a partner.

———— ⓐ on the lawn in front of the house

———— ⓑ in the reeds near the lake

———— ⓒ on a staircase in the house

———— ⓓ in an empty room in the tower

———— ⓔ outside the dining room window

———— ⓕ in a church

9 The title of the story comes from an idiomatic expression—a turn of the screw. The expression is used twice in the original story. The first time is in the Prologue. A man called Griffin tells his friends a ghost story. In it a ghost appears to a child. Afterwards someone says:

"*Griffin's story was unusual; it's true. But if the child gives the effect another turn of the screw, what about a story with TWO children?*"

What does he mean? Tick (√) the correct answer. It might help to think about what happens when you turn a screw in a hole.

a a ghost story is more frightening if the ghost appears to more than one child

b a ghost story is less frightening if the ghost appears to more than one child

10 The extracts below are from different chapters in the story. Look at the Contents on page 3. Which chapters do you think the extracts are from? Write the number of the chapter in the box.

a

They can destroy the children!
They don't know how yet, but they're trying hard.

b

She was standing in the reeds and watching us.

c

YOU must leave Bly, Mrs. Grose.
Take Flora to her uncle in London.

d

I understood immediately that he was looking for somebody!

Prologue

It was Christmas Eve and I was with some friends in an old house in the country. After an early dinner, we lit the candles in the sitting room and gathered[1] around the fire.

"This old house makes me think of ghost stories," Griffin said.

"Oh, please tell us one!" cried the ladies.

"Are you sure?" Griffin asked. "You might be frightened!"

We all agreed that a little excitement was exactly what we wanted, so Griffin started to tell us a story.

When he finished it, nobody moved or spoke for a few moments. Then one of the ladies said, "How unusual! A child that sees a ghost. I haven't heard a story like that before."

After that a couple of other people told stories, but they were rather dull[2].

I noticed that Douglas was very quiet. "He wants to tell us something," I thought.

I was right. Just before we went to bed he said, "Griffin's story was unusual; it's true. But if the child gives the effect another turn of the screw[3], what about a story with TWO children?"

---

1 gather [ˈgæðɚ] (v.) 聚集
2 dull [dʌl] (a.) 乏味的
3 turn of the screw 雪上加霜的行為或事件（因而讓人不得不採取行動）

Of course everyone wanted to hear it.

"I can't tell it. It must be read," said Douglas. "But the story is in a locked drawer in my house in London."

When he saw the looks of disappointment on our faces, he quickly added, "If you like I'll write to my servant in the morning. I can give him the key to the drawer and ask him to send the pages of the story here."

"Did you write the story, Douglas?" I asked.

"No, I didn't," he replied. "It was written by a woman, my sister's governess. She sent me the pages more than twenty years ago, just before she died. She was a charming person, ten years older than me. I met her one summer during the holidays. I was at university at the time. We often went for walks together. I think she liked me and I liked her. I was the only person she told her story to."

The story arrived a few days later. In the evening we all gathered in the sitting room again. Everyone was looking forward to[1] hearing the story. Douglas sat in the best chair next to the fire. The manuscript[2] was on his knees.

"Before you hear the story, you need to know the circumstances[3]," he began. "The woman was the youngest daughter of a poor country priest[4]. Needing to work, she decided to answer an advertisement[5] in a newspaper for the position of governess. The advertiser[6] replied saying that he would like to meet her. Could she come to London?

---

1 look forward to
   期待 (後接名詞或動名詞)
2 manuscript ['mænjə‚skrɪpt] (n.) 原稿
3 circumstances ['sɝkəm‚stænsɪz]
   (n.)〔複〕情況

4 priest [prist] (n.) 神職人員；牧師
5 advertisement [‚ædvɚ'taɪzmənt]
   (n.) (徵人) 啟事；廣告
6 advertiser ['ædvɚ‚taɪzɚ]
   (n.) 刊登啟事者

"She immediately bought a coach[1] ticket and a week later she was on her way there. The advertiser had a big house in a rich part of the city. As she waited at the door she felt both excited and nervous. She was only twenty at the time and this was her first job. A maid[2] let her in and asked her to wait in a small room.

"A few minutes later the master of the house arrived and greeted her. His appearance surprised her. Young, handsome and well-dressed, he was like the men in old romantic novels—or the dreams of a country priest's daughter! She supposed[3] that he was also very rich because the house was full of beautiful things. He sat down opposite[4] her and explained his situation.

"'I'm looking for[5] a governess for my young niece and nephew,' he said and smiled at her.

"'Their parents, my brother and his wife, died two years ago in India and now the children are all alone in the world. I've tried to help the poor little things, but, not being married myself, I have no experience of children. I sent them to live in Bly, my house in Essex. The country is much safer than the city and the air is better. Don't you agree?'

"The young woman nodded[6]. Without knowing why, she really wanted to help him. He was so very charming.

---

1 coach [kotʃ] (n.) 四輪大馬車
2 maid [med] (n.) 女僕
3 suppose [sə'poz] (v.) 猜想；認為應該
4 opposite ['ɑpəzɪt] (prep.) 在對面
5 look for 尋找
6 nod [nɑd] (v.) 點頭
7 housekeeper ['haʊs,kipɚ] (n.) 女管家
8 responsible [rɪ'spɑnsəbl̩] (a.) 負責任的

"'Mrs. Grose, the housekeeper[7] at Bly,' he continued, 'is an excellent woman and there are plenty of servants there. Unfortunately the children's first governess died suddenly. She was a nice young lady and the children loved her. After that we sent Miles to school and Mrs. Grose looked after Flora. You will look after Flora and when Miles comes home for the school holidays, you will be responsible[8] for both of them of course.'"

The Master of the House

- What is the master of the house like?
- Is he interested in the children?
- Does the young woman like him?
- Is he going to offer[9] her the job? Tell a friend.

"He offered her a good salary[10], but she wasn't sure that she wanted the job. She was afraid that she might be lonely in the country with only two children for company[11]."

"But she accepted the job," I said.

"Yes, she did," replied Douglas.

"Because she was in love with[12] the man."

"She saw him only twice."

"It only takes a moment to fall in love[13]," I replied.

---

9   offer [ˈɔfɚ] (v.) 提供
10 salary [ˈsælərɪ] (n.) 薪水
11 company [ˈkʌmpənɪ] (n.) 陪伴
12 be in love with sb 愛上某人
13 fall in love 墜入情網

Douglas got up and moved a log[1] on the fire.

"Yes, you're right," he said. He was looking at the burning logs. "Love is strange, isn't it? She accepted the job knowing that she could never see him again."

"How did she know that?"

"It was one of the conditions of the job. His most important condition. 'If you accept,' he said, 'you will be responsible for the children. You must do everything for them. You mustn't write to me or try to get in touch with[2] me. I don't want to know anything. Do you agree to my condition?'

'I do,' she replied."

"What's the title of the story, Douglas?" somebody asked quietly.

"It hasn't got one," he said sitting down. Then he opened the faded[3] red cover of the manuscript and he began to read.

1 log [lɔg] (n.) 圓木；原木
2 get in touch with sb 聯繫某人
3 faded ['fedɪd] (a.) 褪了色的
4 fly [flaɪ] (n.) 舊時的馬車
5 coach stop 驛站
6 lawn [lɔn] (n.) 草坪
7 in circles （繞）圈子
8 curl [kɜl] (n.) 捲髮
9 expression [ɪk'sprɛʃən] (n.) 表情
10 think of 想到
11 journey ['dʒɜnɪ] (n.) 旅程
12 chat [tʃæt] (v.) 聊天

1. Bly

A fly[4] was waiting for me at the coach stop[5] in Essex.

It was a lovely June evening and I enjoyed the drive through the beautiful countryside to Bly.

The house was a very pleasant building, not the sad place I imagined. There was a lawn[6] at the front and lots of flowers. Birds were flying in circles[7] above the tops of the trees in a clear blue sky. I no longer had any doubts about the job. "You made the right decision," I told myself. "You'll be happy here."

The housekeeper and the little girl appeared at the door to welcome me. I noticed immediately that the child was extremely beautiful. She had golden curls[8], blue eyes and a sweet expression[9] on her little face. She made me think of[10] the angels in old Italian paintings.

"You must be thirsty after your long journey[11], miss," Mrs. Grose said with a smile. "Come in and have some tea!"

She took me to the dining room and we spent the next hour chatting[12] happily. She was a kind, friendly woman and I liked her immediately. "I'm sure we're going to be good friends," I thought.

After tea she showed me my room. It was at the front of the house, so there was a wonderful view of the garden from the windows.

"It's the best room in the house," she told me.

"It's lovely," I said. "And so big!"

There was another, smaller bed at the end of mine.

"That must be for Flora," I said.

"Yes, but I've told her that she can sleep in my room tonight, miss," said Mrs. Grose. "I hope you don't mind. She doesn't know you yet. I thought that she might be worried about sharing a room with a stranger. Is that alright?"

"Thank you, Mrs. Grose," I replied. "That's a very good idea."

The housekeeper's obvious[1] love for the little girl made me like her even more.

Later that evening while we were having supper I asked her about Flora's brother.

"Does he look like an angel too?" I asked.

"Oh, yes, miss!" she answered smiling. "He's just as beautiful as Flora!"

"He's coming home tomorrow, isn't he?"

"Not tomorrow, miss. Friday."

"I'll go and meet him at the coach stop," I said. "And Flora can come too. Do you think he'll like that, Mrs. Grose?"

"Oh, yes," she said. "That's a very good idea."

I was happy that we agreed about everything. I think she respected[2] me because I was the governess. She also seemed VERY glad that I was there.

1 obvious [ˈɑbvɪəs] (a.) 明顯的
2 respect [rɪˈspɛkt] (v.) 尊重；尊敬

That night I was too excited to sleep. I couldn't believe my good luck. Flora was so pretty and so charming! And she was a clever little girl too. "Teaching her will be a pleasure," I thought.

I finally fell asleep, but I woke up several times during the night. Each time I could see Flora's beautiful little face in my head. Once I thought I heard a child's cry and a light footstep[1] outside my room.

"Don't be silly!" I told myself. "You were dreaming. Go back to sleep!"

The next morning I decided to ask my pupil to take me on a tour of the garden and the house. I felt too agitated[2] to start lessons immediately. Bly frightened me a little. It was so different from my own home. I also thought it was a good way of getting to know Flora better.

She was delighted[3] with my suggestion and we started our tour in the garden immediately after breakfast. She took me to see every corner, every tree and every flower in it. We chatted happily all the time and after half an hour we were good friends.

Although she was very young, she wasn't a shy child. She was also very sure of herself and she wasn't afraid of anything. She went into every dark corner and every empty[4] room in the house. She ran up narrow staircases[5]. She stood on the top of the tower. In her blue dress and with her golden hair, she reminded me of[6] a little fairy[7].

That evening after dinner a maid brought me a letter. I opened it and found a short note from my employer[8] and another letter.

The note said:

This letter is from the headmaster[9] of Miles' school—a very boring person. Read what he says, please. Deal with[10] him yourself. Don't contact me! I'm going away.

---

1 footstep ['fʊt,stɛp] (n.) 腳步聲
2 agitated ['ædʒə,tetɪd] (a.) 激動的
3 delighted [dɪ'laɪtɪd] (a.) 高興的
4 empty ['ɛmptɪ] (a.) 空的
5 staircase ['stɛr,kes] (n.) 樓梯;樓梯間
6 remind sb of sth 使某人想到某事

7 fairy ['fɛrɪ] (n.) 仙子;精靈
8 employer [ɪm'plɔɪɚ] (n.) 雇主
9 headmaster ['hɛd'mæstɚ] (n.) 校長
10 deal with sb 想辦法與某人交涉
（尤其指工作上的事務）

I took the headmaster's letter to my room and read it before going to bed. Afterwards I was sorry because the contents gave me a second sleepless[1] night. The next morning I was tired and nervous when I got up. I didn't know what to do about the letter. Finally, I decided to show it to Mrs. Grose.

"Dismissed[2]!" she repeated after I read the headmaster's letter to her. "I don't understand. What does he mean? Aren't all of the boys . . .?"

"Sent home? Yes, they are. But only for the holidays," I replied. "Dismissed means that Miles can't go back to that school—ever! The headmaster doesn't want him. He says that Miles isn't good for the other boys."

Schools

- The words below all describe different kinds of schools in the UK. Write a sentence about each one. Use your dictionary if necessary.
  - boarding
  - public
  - mixed
  - secondary
  - nursery
  - comprehensive

"Master Miles!" the housekeeper said angrily. "How can they say such cruel things? He's only ten years old!"

"It IS difficult to believe," I said.

The expression on her face changed. She was happy that I agreed with her.

"Has he ever behaved badly at home?" I asked.

"He's a boy, miss," she replied laughing. "All boys are bad sometimes. But see him first. Then decide if he's bad or not."

The following day Flora and I got ready to go and meet Miles at the coach stop. While we were waiting for the fly to arrive, I asked Mrs. Grose about the last governess.

"What was she like?"

"She was young and pretty," she replied. "Almost as young and pretty as you!"

"Did she die here?"

"No, miss. She went away."

"Do you mean she was ill and went home to die?"

"No, she wasn't ill here. She left Bly at the end of the year and went home for a short holiday. But she never came back. Then the master told us that she was dead."

"What did she die of[3]?"

"The master never told me, miss," said Mrs. Grose. "But please, miss. If you don't mind I must get back to my work."

---

1 sleepless [ˈsliplɪs] (a.) 失眠的
2 dismiss [dɪsˈmɪs] (v.) 解散；退學
3 die of . . . 死於……原因

2. The face at the window

Miles was waiting for us at the coach stop. Mrs. Grose was right. He was just as beautiful as his sister and even more charming. There was an innocent[1] expression in his blue eyes that I have never seen in a child since then. During the drive back to Bly he completely won my heart.

As soon as[2] I had a free moment, I went to see Mrs. Grose.

"The headmaster's letter is very silly!" I said. "Have you ever met a sweeter child than Miles?"

"Never, miss," she replied with a triumphant[3] smile. She was pleased that I loved Miles as much as she did. "So what are you going to do about the letter, miss?"

"Nothing!" I replied. "I'm not going to write to his uncle and I'm not going to say anything to Miles."

She took my hand and held it for a long time before saying, "I'll stand by[4] you, miss."

I was so grateful[5] to her that I put my arms around her and kissed her cheek.

The next few weeks passed pleasantly. I was always busy with the children during the day, but I had an hour for myself when they went to bed. This was my favorite moment of the day. The summer evenings were long, so I usually went out into the garden.

1　innocent [`ɪnəsn̩t] (a.) 天真無邪的
2　as soon as 一⋯⋯就⋯⋯
3　triumphant [traɪ`ʌmfənt] (a.) 勝利的
4　stand by sb 支持某人
5　grateful [`gretfəl] (a.) 感激的

As I walked in the fading[1] evening light, I often thought about my employer. I was doing what he asked me to do, and I was doing it well. I felt pleased with myself. I imagined meeting him on the garden path. I imagined seeing his face, his smile—a smile that said he approved[2] of me.

I was enjoying my walk one evening when something strange happened. As usual I was thinking about my employer. His handsome face was very clear in my mind. Then, suddenly, I saw him! He wasn't standing on the path in front of me, but on top of the tower in the distance[3].

I gasped[4] twice. Once with shock and then again with surprise. But, no! It wasn't him! It was another man! We looked at each other for several minutes. I wanted to speak to him, but he was too far away. Then, with his eyes still on me, he walked to the other side of the tower and disappeared.

I felt frightened, confused[5] and angry. Who was he? What was he doing there? Was there a "secret" at Bly?

I walked a bit more and when I got back to my room I was calmer[6].

"He was probably just a curious traveler. Someone who wanted to see the park and the house at sunset," I told myself. "Anyway he's gone now. That's the important thing."

I tried to forget the man and concentrate on my work. It wasn't difficult because I enjoyed it so much. Miles and Flora filled every moment of the day with happiness.

---

1 fading ['fedɪŋ] (a.) 變暗的
2 approve [ə'pruv] (v.) 贊同；贊許
3 in the distance 在遠處
4 gasp [gæsp] (v.) 倒抽一口氣
5 confused [kən'fjuzd] (a.) 困惑的
6 calm [kɑm] (a.) 鎮定的

They were both such lovely children. Miles especially was a very sensitive[1] child. He never spoke about his school and I never mentioned it. But I was more certain than ever that the headmaster was wrong. The boy was too innocent to be bad, and schools were cruel places for sensitive children.

A few days later I saw the man again. It was Sunday afternoon and Mrs. Grose and I were getting ready to go to church. I couldn't find my gloves anywhere. Then I remembered that they were in the dining room. I ran downstairs quickly to get them because I didn't want to be late. I opened the door and looked around. It was a gray, wet day, but there was enough light in the room for me to see my gloves on a chair near the window—and somebody outside! It was him! The man from the tower!

My heart missed a beat. He stared[2] at my face for a few seconds and then he disappeared. I understood immediately that he was looking for somebody! But it wasn't me. He wanted somebody else. Suddenly I no longer felt afraid of him.

I ran out of the house and into the garden, but there was no-one there. I looked around but I was sure the man wasn't hiding in the trees or the bushes[3]. I can't explain why.

Then I put my face on the glass of the window and looked into the dining room. I could see Mrs. Grose at the door. When she saw me she turned and hurried away. A few moments later she was running towards me.

"What's the matter?" she cried. "You're as white as a sheet! You look awful!"

As White as a Sheet

- Complete the similes/comparisons with your own ideas. Share your ideas with the class.
  - as black as . . .
  - as cold as . . .
  - as brave as . . .
  - as hungry as . . .

"I saw a man at the window," I said. "I was very frightened."

"Where is he now?" she asked.

"I don't know," I replied.

"Have you seen him before?"

"Yes, once. On the tower."

"Did you recognize[4] him?"

"No, he was a stranger."

"What was he doing on the tower?"

"Only standing and looking down at me."

"You didn't tell me about him. Was he a gentleman?"

I didn't have to think before I answered, "No, not a gentleman. He was a HORROR!"

1   sensitive [ˈsɛnsətɪv] (a.) 靈敏的；敏感的
2   stare [stɛr] (v.) 盯；凝視
3   bush [buʃ] (n.) 灌木叢
4   recognize [ˈrɛkəɡˌnaɪz] (v.) 認出

"A horror! What do you mean?" she said.

I could see that she was frightened too. She turned quickly and looked around the garden, but it was too dark to see anything now.

Then she said suddenly, "It's time to go to church."

"I'm not going," I replied. "I can't leave the children alone."

"Are you afraid . . .?" Mrs. Grose didn't want to say the words that she was thinking.

". . . that he might come back?" I said. "Yes, I am."

The housekeeper didn't say anything, but there was an anxious[1] look on her face.

"She knows something about this man," I thought.

After a short pause[2] she asked, "What does he look like?"

"He has curly red hair and a long pale[3] face," I replied. "His eyes are small and they stare in a strange way. He looks like an actor. You know, tall and straight. But he isn't a gentleman. Oh, no! Not a gentleman!"

"What was he wearing?"

"Smart clothes, but they weren't his own."

She pressed her hands together and looked away. "They're the master's!" she said.

"So you DO know him?"

She didn't answer immediately, and then she cried, "Quint!"

"Quint?"

19 "Peter Quint. He was the master's servant," explained Mrs. Grose. "They were both here last year. Some of the master's clothes disappeared. I suspected[4] Quint but the master didn't say anything. Then the master went away. Quint stayed."

"Alone?"

"Yes. Alone with US." She looked down at her hands. "He was in charge of us."

"And what happened to him?"

After a long silence she finally said, "He went, too."

"Where?"

She looked at me in surprise. "I don't know," she said.

Then after a long pause, "He died."

"Died?" I almost shrieked[5].

"Yes. Mr. Quint is dead!"

---

1 anxious [ˋæŋkʃəs] (a.) 焦慮的
2 pause [pɔz] (n.) 暫停
3 pale [pel] (a.) 蒼白的
4 suspect [səˋspɛkt] (v.) 懷疑；察覺
5 shriek [ʃrik] (v.) 尖叫；喊叫

3. The lady at the lake

[20] It was too late to go to church, so Mrs. Grose and I went back inside and continued our conversation in the schoolroom[1].

"You say that he was looking for somebody," the housekeeper said.

"For Miles," I replied. "He was looking for Miles."

"But how do you know?"

"I know!" I exclaimed[2]. "And YOU know it too, Mrs. Grose! We must protect[3] the children. Will you help me?"

The good woman agreed. She believed what I told her. She didn't think that I was mad.

"It's strange that the children never talk about him," I said.

"Flora probably doesn't remember him," she said. "But Miles spent a lot of time with Quint. They were 'great friends.' That's what Quint said anyway. Quint did what he wanted with Miles. He did what he wanted with everyone."

"So he was a bad person," I said.

"I knew he was, but the master didn't," she replied.

"Why didn't you tell him?"

"He didn't want to know," she said. "He doesn't like trouble. Anyway he trusted Quint. That's why he put him in charge of all of us—including the children."

"How awful!" I cried.

"It was," she said and she burst into tears[4].

I couldn't sleep that night. I kept thinking about Quint. I was sure that Mrs. Grose knew more about the man, but she didn't want to tell me.

When we met during the following days I encouraged her to talk about him.

"He stayed at Bly for several months after the master left," she said. "Then one winter morning his body was found on the road to the village. It seems that he fell on the ice and hit his head. Some people said he was drunk[5] at the time."

"Do you believe that story?" I asked.

"Peter Quint was a bad man with many bad habits," she said. "His past life was full of secrets. We'll never know for sure how he died."

I realized then that my job was more difficult than I thought. The children were alone in the world and they were in great danger. I was the only person who could protect them. I needed to be very brave—heroic[6]! This didn't worry me at all. It was a wonderful opportunity for me to win my employer's respect.

I started to spend more time with the children. I was waiting for something to happen. Sometimes the suspense[7] was almost too much for me. I thought that I might go mad. Then one afternoon it was broken.

---

1   schoolroom [ˈskulˌrum] (n.) 教室
2   exclaim [ɪksˈklem] (v.) 呼喊；驚叫
3   protect [prəˈtɛkt] (v.) 保護
4   burst into tears 突然哭出來
5   drunk [drʌŋk] (a.) 喝醉酒的
6   heroic [hɪˈroɪk] (a.) 英勇的
7   suspense [səˈspɛns] (n.) 掛慮；懸疑

(22) Flora and I were in the garden. The sun was hot that day, so my young pupil and I were in a shady[1] spot near the lake. We were playing a game that Flora invented. Both children were very good at this. I never had to use my own imagination to amuse[2] them.

The lake was the Sea of Azof (we were studying it in our geography[3] lessons) and we were both characters[4] in Flora's story.

She was talking to herself and I was sewing when I suddenly had a feeling that we were not alone. I raised my eyes. There was someone on the other side of the Sea of Azof! A woman. I could see her very clearly.

She was standing in the reeds[5] and watching us. At first I thought she was a servant from the house, or someone from the village. It wasn't unusual to see tradespeople[6] at Bly. I looked at Flora. She was only a short distance away from me now.

"She'll recognize her," I thought. "She'll be able to tell me who she is."

I held my breath while I waited for her to recognize the woman and cry out in alarm. But nothing came. Then, and this was the most frightening thing of all, she turned her back to the lake and continued her game quietly. I watched her. She was concentrating on making a little boat from a piece of wood and a stick.

---

1 shady ['ʃedɪ] (a.) 陰涼的
2 amuse [ə'mjuz] (v.) 消遣
3 geography [dʒɪ'ɑgrəfɪ] (n.) 地理
4 character ['kærɪktɚ] (n.)（故事中的）角色
5 reed [rid] (n.) 蘆葦
6 tradespeople ['tredz,pipl̩] (n.)〔複〕零售商

As soon as I got back to the house, I went to look for Mrs. Grose.

"They KNOW!" I cried throwing my arms around her. "It's horrible. They know! They know!"

"What?" she said, surprised by my emotional[1] behavior.

"What WE know! And perhaps more!"

I pulled myself away and made a big effort[2] to stay calm. "Two hours ago—in the garden!" I explained. "Flora SAW!"

"Did she tell you?" the housekeeper asked anxiously.

"No. She kept it to herself[3]. Just think of it! A child of eight!" I still found it difficult to believe.

The Governess

- Why is the governess so upset?
- What does she find difficult to believe?
- Does she know who the woman in the reeds is?

"Then how do you know?" asked Mrs. Grose.

"I was there! I saw her with my own eyes. Flora knew!"

"Do you mean she saw HIM?"

"Not HIM!" I said. "HER!"

My words shocked the housekeeper.

"Another person," I continued. "A woman in a black dress. A horrible, evil person! She was standing on the other side of the lake."

"Did you recognize her?"

"No, but Flora did. You've seen her too, Mrs. Grose. It was the last governess!"

"Miss Jessel?"

"Yes. Miss Jessel!" I cried. "She was staring at Flora. Oh! The look in her eyes was terrible!"

Mrs. Grose said nothing. She waited for me to explain.

"She wants Flora!" I cried. "I saw it in her eyes. And Flora knows it!"

The housekeeper turned pale and walked to the window. "You say that she was dressed in black," she said in a quiet voice.

"Yes," I said. "And she was beautiful—yes, very beautiful but evil!"

Mrs. Grose slowly came back to me.

"Yes, Miss Jessel was evil," she said taking my hands in hers and pressing them tightly⁴. "Like Quint. They were both evil."

"You must tell me everything you know about these two people now, Mrs. Grose. Was there something between them? Were they lovers?"

"Yes, they were."

"Although he was just . . ."

---

1 emotional [ɪˈmoʃənl] (a.) 感情的；情緒的
2 effort [ˈɛfət] (n.) 努力
3 keep it to oneself 保守祕密
4 tightly [ˈtaɪtlɪ] (adv.) 緊緊地

"... just a servant and she was a lady? Yes." Then she added bitterly[1], "But he didn't care. He didn't have respect for anyone."

"What an awful man!"

"In the end she had to leave. She couldn't stay here."

"What did she die of, Mrs. Grose?"

"I don't know. And I don't want to know," she said.

Then after a short pause she added softly, "Afterwards I imagined. I still imagine. But what I imagine is too awful to say."

I burst into tears when I heard that.

"I wanted to save the children!" I sobbed[2]. "But it's too late! They're already lost!"

4. A bad boy

(26) Later that evening Mrs. Grose came to my room and we had another long talk. She agreed with me that the ghosts must be real. My descriptions[3] of Quint and Miss Jessel were perfect. Now we were both worried about the children. What did they know? Were they hiding something from us?

"I can't believe they are bad children," I said. "They're so good when they're with me."

Then I remembered Mrs. Grose's words when the headmaster's letter arrived: "All boys are bad sometimes." I reminded her of this and asked her about it.

"What did you mean?" I asked. "Tell me about it, my dear. I must know everything."

She hesitated[4]. I waited patiently for her to begin.

"Well," she said finally. "For several months Miles and Quint spent a lot of time together. Too much time, in my opinion[5]. I mentioned it to Miss Jessel, but she wasn't interested. One day I said something to Miles about it. I tried to explain to him that it wasn't a good thing for a gentleman to spend so much time with a servant, but . . ."

She blushed[6] and looked away from me. I finished the sentence for her.

1   bitterly [ˈbɪtəlɪ] (adv.) 激烈地
2   sob [sɑb] (v.) 嗚咽；啜泣
3   description [dɪˈskrɪpʃən] (n.) 敘述

4   hesitate [ˈhɛzəˌtet] (v.) 猶豫
5   opinion [əˈpɪnjən] (n.) 意見
6   blush [blʌʃ] (v.) 臉紅

27

"... but he said that you were a servant too."

"Yes. He also denied[1] being with Quint on certain afternoons. But I knew that they were together."

"So he lied to you," I said. "That isn't like Miles."

In the days that followed I watched the children all the time. Did they suspect why? Did they understand that I only wanted to protect them from the evil control of Quint and Miss Jessel?

I tried not to show them my fears[2], but sometimes I couldn't stop myself from putting my arms around them and holding them tightly. They became very fond[3] of me at that time. They were always doing things to please me. They worked harder at their lessons. They learnt poems and invented stories for me. They sang songs and Miles learnt to play new pieces on the piano. There was never a dull moment in the schoolroom.

Both children were clever, but Miles was especially quick at learning things. He was good at reading and learnt many things by himself from books. I didn't worry about looking for another school for him. It was a problem that I preferred to forget. Anyway I didn't think that school was the best place for him. It was better for him to be at Bly with Flora. They were very happy together. They never disagreed and they shared all their secrets.

---

1   deny [dɪˋnaɪ] (v.) 否認
2   fear [fɪr] (n.) 害怕；擔心
3   fond [fɑnd] (a.) 喜歡的
4   advantage [ədˋvæntɪdʒ] (n.) 優點

5   disadvantage [ˌdɪsədˋvæntɪdʒ] (n.) 缺點
6   passage [ˋpæsɪdʒ] (n.) 走廊
7   more or less 多少有一點

Home Schooling

- Work with a friend. Talk about home schooling (doing lessons at home with a parent or private teacher, not at a school).
- Why do children sometimes need to do home schooling?
- What are the advantages[4] and disadvantages[5] of learning at home?
- Would you prefer to study at home or at school?

And so the days passed. I didn't have much time for myself, but when I was free I read. There were lots of books at Bly and I always kept one in my room.

One evening I became so interested in the story I was reading that I forgot the time. It was very late when I finally closed my book. At that moment I heard a noise outside my door. Somebody was moving in the house. I put the book down, picked up the candle and went into the passage[6], locking the door quietly behind me.

Holding my candle high, I walked along the passage to the tall window at the top of the staircase.

Then three things happened more or less[7] at the same time. My candle went out, I noticed that it was getting light outside, and I heard someone coming up the stairs. In the pale light from the window I could see the person clearly. It was Quint! He was about halfway up the staircase!

When he saw me he stopped and we looked at each other. We didn't speak although we were very close. It was like meeting a thief in a sleeping house in the middle of the night. He seemed as human as a real person. Only the silence between us was unnatural. Fortunately I didn't feel afraid, and he knew it. We stood looking at each other for a long time. Then he turned and disappeared into the darkness at the bottom of the stairs.

When I was sure that he was no longer there, I walked back along the passage to my room. I unlocked the door quietly and went in.

The first thing I saw was Flora's empty bed. My heart stopped beating for a second. Where was she? Then I heard a noise near the window. She was standing behind the curtain.

"Bad governess!" she said before I could speak. "Where have you been?"

Instead of being angry with her, I felt only relief[1]. I sank[2] into my chair and she immediately ran over to me and sat on my knees. In her nightgown[3] and with her pink cheeks and golden curls, she looked exactly like a little angel.

"Why were you looking out of the window?" I asked. "Did you think that I was in the garden?"

"I got up because I thought that someone was outside," she replied very seriously.

---

1   relief [rɪ'lif] (n.) 輕鬆；寬心
2   sink [sɪŋk] (v.) 下沉（動詞三態：sink; sank/sunk; sunk/sunken）
3   nightgown ['naɪt,gaʊn] (n.) 睡衣

(30) "And did you see anyone?"

She hesitated for just a second before replying, "No."

I immediately thought that she was lying. I don't know why. Perhaps because I was feeling so nervous. I wanted to say, "Who did you see? Tell me the truth! You know that I know, don't you!"

But I didn't. Instead I stood up and said, "Why did you pull the curtains around your bed? To make me believe that you were still there?"

She gave me one of her sweetest smiles and said, "Because I didn't want to frighten you."

Every night after that I stayed awake until very late. When I was sure that Flora was asleep, I left the room quietly. I went to the top of the stairs, but I never saw Quint again. I saw Miss Jessel there once. She was sitting on the bottom step with her head in her hands. I thought she was crying. Then suddenly, without turning round, she disappeared.

Ghosts

- Work with a friend. What are ghosts?
- Can they hurt people?
- Can everyone see them?

On the eleventh night I decided to go to bed early because I was very tired. I fell asleep immediately, but I woke up at about one o'clock in the morning. There was no light in the room and my first thought was, "Flora has blown out[1] the candle."

I jumped out of bed and lit the candle again. Flora wasn't in her bed. She was standing at the window looking out into the night. She didn't notice that I was awake, so I was sure that she could see something—or someone—in the garden below.

"It must be Miss Jessel," I thought.

I opened the door quietly and went into the passage. I wanted to know what Flora could see. I had to find another window that had a view of the garden. I listened at Miles' door for a moment, but I heard nothing. I hurried to an empty room in the tower, opened the window and looked down at the lawn below. I could see a person looking in my direction—not at me, but above me.

"There must be somebody at the window upstairs," I thought. The light from the moon was bright enough for me to see the person in the garden very clearly. I felt sick when I recognized him. It was poor little Miles!

1 blow out 吹熄

5. Dangerous friends

I didn't call him because I didn't want to wake up everyone in the house. Instead I went quickly downstairs and into the garden. He didn't say anything when he saw me. He just came up to me and let me take him back inside.

When we got to his room, I put my hands on his shoulders and looked at him very seriously.

"Miles, you must tell me the truth now. Why did you go out?"

He smiled at me and at that moment in the moonlight he looked like a little fairy prince.

"If I tell you why, will you understand?"

I nodded.

"Well," he said sweetly, "I wanted to show you that I could be a BAD boy sometimes!"

Then he moved forward and kissed me. I was so surprised by both his answer and his kiss that I almost started to cry. I put my arms around him and kissed him back. I couldn't speak.

"I didn't take my clothes off when I came to bed," he explained pulling himself free of my arms. "I sat and read until midnight. Then I went downstairs. You see, when I'm bad, I'm VERY bad!"

"And how did you plan to wake me up?" I asked.

"I told Flora to get up and look out of the window," he went on as sweetly as before. "The noise woke you up. You wanted to know what she was looking at. So you looked and you saw me."

"Catching cold[1] in the night air!" I said, trying to be angry.

He laughed. "Yes," he replied, "I WAS bad, wasn't I?"

I could see that he was proud of himself. I didn't know what to say to him, so I kissed him again and left the room.

I had to wait until the evening of the following day before I could speak to Mrs. Grose. I was so glad that I could share my worries and secrets with her. Talking to her always made me feel better. She listened patiently to everything I told her. She didn't have much imagination herself. She only saw how beautiful, how sweet and how clever the children were.

The sun was still warm, so I invited her to sit with me for a while in the garden. The children were walking up and down the lawn not far from us. Miles was reading a story to Flora. Mrs. Grose was watching them as she listened to me. There was a happy smile on her face.

I started to describe the night's events to her, but she wasn't very interested. She didn't seem to understand the seriousness of the situation.

She only gave me her full attention[2] when I said, "But the truth is in the last thing that Miles said to me."

"What was that?" she asked.

"'You don't know how bad I CAN be!'" I looked at the housekeeper triumphantly. "Miles knows very well how bad he can be, of course. And the headmaster at his school knows too."

"But you said that the headmaster's letter was silly!" said Mrs. Grose a little angrily. "Have you changed your opinion of the child?"

"No, I haven't," I replied. "I'm just beginning to understand what is happening here at Bly."

"And what IS happening?"

---

1 catch cold 著涼   2 attention [əˋtɛnʃən] (n.) 注意

(34) "I'm sure that the four of them—Miles, Flora, Miss Jessel and Quint—meet very often. Look at the children now! They look very sweet and innocent, don't they? But they're deceiving[1] us all the time. Miles isn't reading a fairy story to Flora. He's talking to her about THEM! Those two ghosts!"

The children were walking up and down the lawn. I could see from Mrs. Grose's expression that she found my words difficult to believe.

"When I first met the children," I went on, "I thought that they were very unusual. I couldn't explain why, but now I can. Those children aren't like ordinary[2] children. They're too beautiful and too good. But they're deceiving us. They're just playing a game. They haven't been good—they've only been absent."

Mrs. Grose didn't say anything. She just stared at me.

What Do You Think?

- Does Mrs. Grose believe the governess?
- If Miles and Flora are playing a game, why are they playing it?
- What are "ordinary children" like? Share your ideas with the class.

---

1 deceive [dɪˈsiv] (v.) 欺騙
2 ordinary [ˈɔrdn̩ˌɛrɪ] (a.) 平常的；普通的

"I know it seems mad, but it's true." I replied. "They don't belong to us. They're not mine—they're not ours. They're his and they're hers!"

"Quint's and that woman's?"

"Yes! They want to possess[1] the children."

This was almost too much for Mrs. Grose.

"But why?" she asked looking back at the children. "Why do they want those poor little things?"

"Because they want to continue their evil ways with them!"

"Evil ways!" Mrs. Grose's face turned pale. "What evil ways?"

"During those months that they were alone with the children," I explained, "they filled the children with evil. They want to continue their evil work because it will bring them back to this world."

"Oh, dear!" exclaimed Mrs. Grose. "What terrible people! But what can they do now?"

"Do?" I almost shouted.

The children heard me and stopped. They smiled at us, waved[2] their hands and went on walking.

"They can destroy[3] the children! They don't know how yet, but they're trying hard. At the moment they appear in strange places—on the top of the tower, on the other side of the lake, outside windows. But soon they will succeed and . . ."

". . . the children will try to go to them . . ." Mrs. Grose whispered[4].

". . . and will die doing it!"

Mrs. Grose stood up and walked a short distance away from me.

"So we have to stop them," I said. "Before they hurt the children."

My friend didn't say anything for a long time. She stood looking at the garden. I knew that she was thinking hard about what to do.

Finally she said, "Their uncle must do something to stop them. He must take the children away."

"And who's going to tell him?" I asked.

She turned and looked at me. "You are, miss."

"But he told me never to get in touch with him about anything."

Mrs. Grose followed the children with her eyes for a few moments. Then she came back to her chair and sat down. Taking my arm she said, "But you must MAKE him come. He should be here. He should help us."

We looked at each other. She knew my thoughts.

"If I write he'll laugh at me. He won't respect me anymore. He'll think that I'm just trying to attract[5] his attention."

Women understand each other.

"I CAN'T write to him," I said. "And if YOU write to him and say anything . . .,"

She was frightened of me now.

". . . I'll leave Bly immediately."

---

1 possess [pəˋzɛs] (v.) 掌握；支配
2 wave [wev] (v.) 揮；揮手表示
3 destroy [dɪˋstrɔɪ] (v.) 毀壞；殺死
4 whisper [ˋhwɪspɚ] (v.) 低聲說
5 attract [əˋtrækt] (v.) 吸引

6. A difficult decision

The weeks passed and the summer ended. With the start of autumn the weather changed. The skies were gray every day and it was cold and wet. I often thought about asking the children about Quint and Miss Jessel during those weeks, but I never had the courage.

One Sunday morning while we were on our way to church Miles suddenly asked me, "When am I going back to school?"

His question took me by surprise. I had no answer ready.

Seeing my confusion[1], he continued talking. "You know, it isn't good for a boy to be with a lady ALWAYS. You're a very nice lady of course, but I'm a boy and I'm getting older."

"Yes, you are," I finally managed to[2] say.

"So when am I going back?"

"Were you happy at school?" I asked.

"I'm happy everywhere."

"Well, if that's true, stay at Bly!"

"But I want to see more of life." Then he added, "And I want to be with people like me."

We were almost at the church. Mrs. Grose and Flora were already inside.

Just before we reached the door, Miles asked, "Does my uncle know that I'm growing up?"

"I don't think that he's very interested."

"So he won't come."

"To Bly? Who will make him?" I asked.

"I will! I'll make him!" said Miles, and he ran into the church.

I didn't follow him. I was too agitated. I walked around the churchyard[3] and thought about our conversation. It was clear to me now that Miles had a plan. He understood that I was afraid to ask his uncle to come to Bly. And he was using my fear to get what he wanted—to return to school.

I suddenly felt afraid of him. I wanted to get away from Bly and forget everything. A voice in my head said, "Go now! Go home and pack your bags while everyone's at church!"

I hesitated. Was it the right thing to do? I had to decide quickly.

"Yes," I thought. "I'll go."

I hurried back across the churchyard and the garden.

When I entered the silent house, I was beginning to feel excited about leaving.

"If you are very quick," I told myself, "you'll be able to get away without a fuss[4]. But you'll have to be very quick!"

But my excitement soon changed to despair[5] when I thought about my escape[6] more carefully. It was a long way to the coach stop. How could I get there without a fly?

---

1 confusion [kənˈfjuʒən] (n.) 困惑
2 manage to 設法
3 churchyard [ˈtʃɜtʃˈyɑrd] (n.) 教堂庭院；教堂墓地

4 fuss [fʌs] (n.) 忙亂；大驚小怪
5 despair [dɪˈspɛr] (n.) 絕望；喪失信心
6 escape [əˈskep] (n.) 逃跑；逃離

1 tragic [`trædʒɪk] (a.) 悲慘的
2 miserable [`mɪzərəbḷ] (a.) 悲哀的
3 suffer [`sʌfɚ] (v.) 遭受；受苦
4 torments [`tɔr͵mɛnts]
　(n.)〔複〕痛苦；苦惱
5 hell [hɛl] (n.) 地獄

I sat down on the stairs and put my head in my hands. Then I remembered Miss Jessel. She was sitting in the same place with her head in her hands when I saw her a month ago! The memory frightened me. I stood up quickly and went upstairs to the schoolroom to collect my things.

I was surprised to see a woman at my desk. She was writing something with my pen. At first I thought it was a servant. Then she stood up and walked across the room. I recognized the black dress, the beautiful face and the tragic[1] expression. It was Miss Jessel!

"You terrible, miserable[2] woman!" I shouted at her.

I thought she heard me because she looked at me for a moment. Then she disappeared. I stood there alone in the sunshine and I knew that I had to stay at Bly.

That afternoon just before tea I went to see Mrs. Grose in her room.

"What happened to you this morning?" she asked. "Why didn't you come to church?"

"I came home to talk to Miss Jessel!"

Mrs. Grose tried not to show her surprise.

"To talk to her? Do you mean that she spoke to you?"

"Well, yes," I said.

"What did she say?"

"She said that she suffers[3] the torments[3] . . ." I stopped. I was almost too afraid to say the words. ". . . of hell[5]!"

Mrs. Grose looked at me in horror.

"She wants to share them with Flora!" I went on. "But you mustn't worry," I added quickly. "I've decided to write to the children's uncle."

"Oh, yes, miss. Please write to him!" the housekeeper said almost in tears.

"Miles thinks that I'm afraid to write to him, but he's wrong. His uncle must know everything now. He must know why I didn't look for another school for the child. I'll show him the letter from the headmaster. I'll tell him that I couldn't find another school for a child who was sent away for . . ."

"We've never known why, miss," Mrs. Grose said.

". . . for being wicked[1]! It can only be THAT, Mrs. Grose! It's his uncle's fault of course. It was very wrong to leave the children with those terrible people."

Mrs. Grose started crying. She didn't want to believe that Miles was a bad boy.

"I'll write the letter this evening," I said.

When the children were in bed I took out my pen and some paper. It was raining heavily outside and the wind was making the windows rattle[2]. I looked at Flora. She was sleeping peacefully. I picked up the candle and went to Miles' room. He was still awake.

"Why aren't you asleep?" I asked.

(41) "I'm lying here and thinking," he replied.

"What are you thinking about?"

"About you," he replied. "About my life here. About how you bring me up³. And all the rest."

"What do you mean?" I asked anxiously.

"You know! You know!" he said with a smile.

We looked at each in other in silence for a moment.

Then I said, "You'll certainly go back to school, Miles. Not to the old place. We'll find a better one for you. Aren't you happy at home?"

"Oh, yes. But I want to get away," he said. "I'm a boy and I want what boys want."

I didn't say anything. What did boys want? I felt that Miles knew much better than I did.

Miles

- What does Miles want? Why?
- Why hasn't the governess found another school for him?
- Do you think Miles will ever go back to school?

---

1 wicked [ˋwɪkɪd] (a.) 壞的；缺德的
2 rattle [ˋrætl] (v.) 發出咯咯聲
3 bring up 養育長大

"My uncle must come to Bly," he said staring at the ceiling. "He must decide what to do."

"I've started to write a letter to him," I said.

"Well, finish it!"

I stood up slowly, but I didn't leave the room. I couldn't.

"What happened before you came back to Bly, Miles?" I asked. "And what happened before you went away?"

He looked at me, but he didn't reply.

"Dear little Miles!" I said putting my arms around him. "I only want to help you. I only want you to help me save you."

At that moment an icy cold wind blew through the room. Miles shrieked loudly and I jumped up. Suddenly I realized that I was standing in the dark.

"Oh, the candle's gone out!" I cried.

"No," said Miles. "I blew it out!"

7. A departure

The next day the children worked harder than usual at their lessons. Miles especially was very kind to me. After lunch he asked me if I would like to hear him play the piano. Perhaps he was sorry for his behavior of the previous day. We went together to the schoolroom and he started to play. I don't think I fell asleep, but I completely forgot about Flora for half an hour. When I remembered her, I jumped up and looked around.

"Where's Flora?" I asked Miles.

He laughed. "I have no idea!" he replied and continued playing.

"She must be with Mrs. Grose," I thought. I hurried downstairs to her room. But she wasn't.

The housekeeper and I looked all over the house for her. We couldn't find her anywhere.

"She's gone out," I said. "She's with HER!"

"And where's Miles?" asked Mrs. Grose.

"He's upstairs in the schoolroom," I replied. "His plan has worked! He found a way to keep me quiet while Flora went to meet Miss Jessel. Now he's free too, so he can meet Quint. But I don't mind."

Mrs. Grose looked at me in surprise. "Have you written the letter?" she asked anxiously.

I took it out of my pocket and put it on the hall[1] table.

"Yes. Luke can post it," I said.

Luke was one of the servants. Then I opened the door and went outside.

"Aren't you going to put a coat on?" Mrs. Grose called.

"I don't have time."

I ran across the lawn towards Flora's favorite place in the garden—the lake. Mrs. Grose followed me.

"She'll be where we saw Miss Jessel," I told the housekeeper. "I've always suspected that she wanted to go back to that place alone. And now her brother has managed to arrange[2] it for her."

But there was no-one there.

I looked for the small boat that the children sometimes took out on the lake.

"The boat's missing!" I cried. "She's taken it and gone to the other side!"

"Alone?" Mrs. Grose replied. "But she's only a child!"

"She's not alone, and when she's with Miss Jessel, she isn't a child. She's an old, old woman," I said. "Come on! We must walk around the lake and find her."

We soon saw the boat. It was hidden in the reeds. But there was no sign of Flora. We walked a bit further. Then we saw her too. She was in a field.

45 "There she is!" we both cried together.

Flora heard us and smiled. We ran up to her and Mrs. Grose immediately threw herself on her knees and hugged the child.

Flora was the first to speak. "Where are your hats and coats?" she asked. "And where's Miles?"

"I'll tell you where Miles is if you tell ME . . ." I heard myself say.

"What?"

Mrs. Grose looked at me and gasped in horror. But she couldn't stop me now.

". . . where Miss Jessel is, my dear!"

Then I saw her. She was standing on the other side of the lake. She was looking straight at us.

"She's there! She's there!" I cried and pointed[3].

I was sure that Mrs. Grose and Flora could see her too. But Flora wasn't looking at the place I was pointing at. She was looking at me with a very serious expression on her little face. It frightened me.

"She's there, you unhappy little thing," I shouted. "There! THERE! You can see her as clearly as you can see me!"

"What can you see, miss?" Mrs. Grose said.

I knew from the expression on her face that she didn't believe me. "Can't you see her?" I cried taking hold of her arm. "Look, dear woman, LOOK!"

---

1 hall [hɔl] (n.) 大廳
2 arrange [əˈrendʒ] (v.) 安排
3 point [pɔɪnt] (v.) 指向

"I can't see anything, miss," she replied coldly.

Then she put her arm around the little girl and held her tightly. "There's nobody there, my sweet." Her voice was kind. "How can poor Miss Jessel be there when she's dead? Come on! Let's go home now!"

Flora was still looking at me. The expression on her face was like a mask. It made her seem hard and ugly.

"I can't see anybody or anything. I never HAVE seen anything," she shouted at me. "I think you're cruel. I don't like you!"

Then she hid her face in Mrs. Grose's dress and cried loudly, "Take me away! Please! Take me away from HER!"

I felt sorry for the child. There was nothing more I could do for her.

"I've done my best to save you," I said, "but I've lost you. Mrs. Grose! Take her back to the house."

Flora

- How was Flora feeling at that moment?
- What did she think of the governess?
- What will happen to Flora now?

I don't remember well what happened after that. I suppose I lay down on the grass[1] and cried. My face was wet when I looked up and it was dark. I walked back and went straight to my room. Flora's bed was no longer there.

The next morning Mrs. Grose woke me up very early with some bad news.

"Flora's ill, miss. She cried all night. She's frightened of you!"

"Has she talked about Miss Jessel?"

"No, miss. She says that she didn't see anyone at the lake."

"Nature made those children clever. Quint and Miss Jessel have made them cleverer. Now Flora will complain² about me to her uncle because she wants to get rid of³ me."

"She never wants to see you again, miss."

"Have you come here to tell me to leave Bly?" I asked. Then, without waiting for her reply I said, "I have a better idea. YOU must leave Bly, Mrs. Grose. Take Flora to her uncle in London. I'll stay here with Miles. I'm sure he wants to tell me something, but he needs more time. Leave as soon as you can."

Mrs. Grose looked a little embarrassed and didn't say anything.

"But perhaps you don't want to go," I said.

"I'll go," she said putting her hand on mine. "I'll go this morning. You're right, miss. I can't stay here."

She suddenly burst into tears.

"She says really terrible things . . .' she sobbed.

"About me?"

"Yes, miss," she said drying her eyes. "The words she uses are really shocking. I don't know where she learnt them." She looked at her watch. "But I must go back to her now."

---

¹ grass [græs] (n.) 草；草地
² complain [kəm'plen] (v.) 抱怨
³ get rid of 擺脫

"Remember! Our employer will have my letter by now," I said. "So he will already know about Miles."

"Your letter never went, miss. Master Miles . . .'

". . . took it?" I gasped.

"Luke didn't post[1] it," she said. "And it wasn't on the table when Flora and I got back." She started crying again. "Perhaps he did that at school too, miss!" she sobbed. "Perhaps he stole letters!"

"Well, there was nothing in MY letter that he didn't already know," I replied. "Don't worry, Mrs. Grose. He'll tell me everything. Now go! Quickly!"

8. Lost forever

When I went downstairs later, the house seemed empty and quiet. I felt anxious and lonely. The servants stared at me, but they didn't ask any questions about the housekeeper's sudden departure[2].

I didn't see Miles all day. He finally arrived at dinner time. I was already in the dining room and the food was on the table. He stood beside me with his hands in his pockets.

"Is she very ill?" he asked.

"Flora? No, not very. She'll get better soon in London. Bly wasn't good for her. Come and sit down. Here's some meat[3] for you."

He took his plate[4] and sat down. We ate our dinner in silence.

When we finished I called the maid and asked her to take everything away. While she was doing this, Miles got up and looked out of the window. As soon as the girl left the room, he turned to me and said, "So! We're alone!"

"More or less." I tried to smile.

He came and stood in front of me.

"Yes," he said. "Of course the others are still here. But they aren't very important, are they?"

---

1 post [post] (v.) 郵寄
2 departure [dɪˋpɑrtʃɚ] (n.) 離開

3 meat [mit] (n.) 肉
4 plate [plet] (n.) 盤；碟

"It depends."

"Yes," he said. "Everything depends!"

He went back to the window and put his head on the glass. He seemed uncomfortable and anxious. Was he looking for something that he couldn't see?

When he finally turned round he said, "Well, I'm glad Bly is good for ME!"

"Have you enjoyed yourself today?"

"Oh, yes. I've walked miles and miles. I've never been so free."

"Do you like it?"

He smiled and then he said, "Do YOU?" Before I could answer he went on, "You're more alone here than I am. Do you mind?"

"Looking after you? No, of course not. That's why I'm still here."

"You've stayed here just for me?"

"Certainly. I'm your friend. Do you remember the night of the storm? I told you that I only wanted to help you."

"Yes, yes." He laughed nervously. "But it was only because you wanted me to do something for you," he added.

"That's true. Do you remember what it was?"

"Oh, yes," he said happily. "You wanted me to tell you something."

"That's right."

"Is THAT why you've stayed here?"

"Well, yes, it is."

He was quiet for a long time. Finally he said, "Must I tell you now? Here?"

"Yes."

Suddenly I had the feeling that he was a little afraid of me.

"Do you want to go out again?" I asked softly.

"Very much." He smiled at me.

I waited.

"Alright. I'll tell you everything," he said. "But not now."

"Why not now?"

"I have to see Luke."

It was a lie and I felt ashamed[1] of making him tell it. I was sorry for him.

The Lie

- What does the governess want to know?
- Why does Miles tell her a lie?
- Why does the governess feel sorry for him?

---

1 ashamed [əˈʃemd] (a.) 感到可恥的
2 soul [sol] (n.) 靈魂

"Well, go to Luke," I said. "I'll wait. But before you leave me, tell me one thing. Did you take my letter yesterday afternoon?"

At that moment the face of Peter Quint suddenly appeared at the window behind Miles! I immediately took hold of the boy and pulled him towards me. I didn't want him to see that horrible person outside. For a few seconds there was a silent fight between Quint and myself for the child's soul[2]. I could feel it strongly.

"Yes, I took it," Miles said in a low voice. His little face was as white as the face at the window.

I put my arms around him and held him close to me. His body was hot and I could feel his heart beating.

"Why did you take it?" I said.

"To see what you said about me."

"Did you open it?"

"Yes," he whispered.

I looked up. I expected to see Quint's face at the window, but it was no longer there. Miles was saved!

"But you found nothing!" I almost shouted with happiness.

"Nothing. So I burned it."

"Miles, did you take letters—or other things—at school? Is that why you can't go back?"

"Did you know that I couldn't go back?" he asked.

"I know everything."

"Everything?"

"Everything. So, did you . . .?" I couldn't say the word.

"Steal? No!"

"What did you do then?"

He took two or three deep breaths. "Well, I said things."

"Who did you say them to?"

He looked confused. "I don't know! I don't remember their names."

"Did you say them to a lot of people?"

"No, only to the people I liked. Then they told other people."

He took another deep breath. His forehead[1] was covered in sweat[2].

"And those people told the headmaster."

"Yes," he said. "I'm surprised he told you about them."

"He didn't. What WERE those things, Miles?"

He turned to look out of the window. At the same moment the horrible white face of Quint appeared again. I felt sick. I took hold of Miles again and hugged him.

"No more, no more!" I shrieked.

"Is she HERE?" Miles gasped. "Miss Jessel?"

"It isn't Miss Jessel," I cried. "Look! THERE!"

Miles was confused. His eyes searched[3] the room for the face that he couldn't see.

1 forehead [ˈfɔr‚hɛd] (n.) 額頭
2 sweat [swɛt] (n.) 汗
3 search [sɜtʃ] (v.) 尋找

"Is it HIM?" he shouted angrily.

"Who?"

"Peter Quint—you devil! WHERE?"

"It doesn't matter[1] now, Miles," I said. "I have you. He has lost you forever. Look! He's THERE!"

Miles turned quickly towards the window. He looked and saw only the quiet day outside. Then he suddenly gave a cry of pain and fell backwards. I caught him and hugged him.

At the end of a minute I realized that his little heart was no longer beating.

1 it doesn't matter 不要緊；沒關係

AFTER READING

Ⓐ Personal Response

1 Answer the questions. Share your ideas with the rest of the class.

- a Did you enjoy reading the story?
- b Did you think it was frightening?
- c Do you think that the children saw the ghosts?
- d Were you surprised by the ending?
- e Would you recommend the story to your friends?
- f Do you think it could work with a modern setting?
- g Would you like to see a film version of the story?

2 Work in small groups. Make a list of films or stories you know with ghosts in them.

3 Decide together which film or story on your list is

- a the most scary.
- b the least scary.

Share your ideas with the rest of the class.

❸ Comprehension

4 Put a tick (√) next to the correct answer.

_____ ⓐ The governess was a doctor's daughter.

⬜**1** True   ⬜**2** False   ⬜**3** Don't Know

_____ ⓑ Bly was a sad, dark place.

⬜**1** True   ⬜**2** False   ⬜**3** Don't Know

_____ ⓒ Mrs. Grose liked her employer.

⬜**1** True   ⬜**2** False   ⬜**3** Don't Know

_____ ⓓ Quint had a secret past.

⬜**1** True   ⬜**2** False   ⬜**3** Don't Know

_____ ⓔ Miss Jessel and Quint were lovers.

⬜**1** True   ⬜**2** False   ⬜**3** Don't Know

_____ ⓕ Miss Jessel left Bly after Quint died.

⬜**1** True   ⬜**2** False   ⬜**3** Don't Know

_____ ⓖ Miles never told lies.

⬜**1** True   ⬜**2** False   ⬜**3** Don't Know

_____ ⓗ Flora went to the lake to see Miss Jessel.

⬜**1** True   ⬜**2** False   ⬜**3** Don't Know

_____ ⓘ Miles wanted to go back to school.

⬜**1** True   ⬜**2** False   ⬜**3** Don't Know

_____ ⓙ Miles died because he saw Quint's face at the window.

⬜**1** True   ⬜**2** False   ⬜**3** Don't Know

5 Read the extracts from the story.
Who do the underlined words refer to?

 [a] I think she liked me and I liked <u>her</u>. _____

 [b] She never saw <u>him</u> again. _____

 [c] <u>They</u> were both here last year. _____

 [d] I felt sick when I recognized <u>him</u>. _____

 [e] She's with <u>HER</u>! _____

6 How many people tell a story in *The Turn of the Screw*?
Who are they? How are their stories connected?

7 Why did Mrs. Grose believe the governess?

8 Why did the governess talk to Miles about his school only
at the end of the story?

9 What did the governess say about the children at these
points in the story? Find the pictures in the book and look
for her words.

C Characters

🔊 **10** Work with a partner. Decide together which word, or words, from the box best describe the characters and say why. You can use the words more than once. You don't need to use all the words.

> amusing   charming   clever   dishonest
> friendly   kind   lazy   romantic
> rude   sad

a the governess _____

b the master of Bly _____

c Mrs. Grose _____

d Miles and Flora _____

e Miss Jessel _____

f Quint _____

11 Who said the following, to whom and when?

a I don't want to know anything.

b Dismissed means that Miles can't go back to that school—ever!

c His past life was full of secrets.

d It's horrible. They know! They know!

e Bad governess!

f You're more alone here than I am.

12 Work with a partner. Discuss the following questions about the governess.

    a Where did she grow up?

    b What did her father do?

    c Why was she looking for a job?

    d Why was she surprised when she first saw her employer?

    e Why did she often think of him when she first arrived at Bly?

    f Why did she want him to approve of her?

    g In what way was she similar to Miss Jessel?

    h Was she mad?

13 Work with a partner. Do you agree or disagree with the following sentences about the children? Explain your opinions.

    a They were sad and lonely.

    b They were good and kind.

14 Answer the questions about Quint and Miss Jessel.

    a Mrs. Grose says that Quint and Miss Jessel were evil. What did they do to make her think this?

    b In reply to the governess's question about the cause of Miss Jessel's death, Mrs. Grose says, "Afterwards I imagined. I still imagine. But what I imagine is too awful to say." What do you think she imagines?

15 Why is the character of Mrs. Grose important in the story?

❶ Plot and Theme

16 Read the pairs of sentences. Which event happened first? Put a tick (√) in the box next to the sentence.

a ☐ 1 The governess received a letter from her employer.
☐ 2 Flora showed the governess around the house and gardens.

b ☐ 1 Mrs. Grose told the governess that Peter Quint was dead.
☐ 2 The governess saw the face of Peter Quint outside the dining room window.

c ☐ 1 The governess saw the ghost of Miss Jessel at the lake.
☐ 2 Mrs. Grose told the governess that Miss Jessel and Quint were lovers.

d ☐ 1 The governess saw the ghosts on the stairs.
☐ 2 Miles went into the garden at midnight.

e ☐ 1 The children worked very hard at their lessons.
☐ 2 The governess told Mrs. Grose that the ghosts wanted to possess the children.

f ☐ 1 Miles talked to the governess about going back to school.
☐ 2 Mrs. Grose asked the governess to write a letter to the master.

g ☐ 1 Miles stole the letter to his uncle.
☐ 2 Flora went to the lake on her own.

h ☐ 1 Mrs. Grose took Flora to London.
☐ 2 Miles talked to the governess about his school.

17 Work with a partner. Suggest possible answers to the questions.

(a) How did the governess know what Quint and Miss Jessel looked like?

(b) Why did Mrs. Grose say that Quint and Miss Jessel were evil?

(c) Why didn't the governess want to ask her employer for help?

(d) Why did Flora become ill after the scene at the lake?

(e) What happened to the governess after Miles died?

18 Match a theme of the story (a–d) with a fact (1–4) that relates to it.

(1) Both Miss Jessel and Peter Quint were young and good-looking.

(2) The governess tried to protect the children from the ghosts because she wanted her employer's respect.

(3) The children looked like angels.

(4) Mrs. Grose didn't approve of Miss Jessel's relationship with Quint.

_____ (a) Physical beauty is often associated with moral goodness.

_____ (b) Evil can hide behind physical beauty.

_____ (c) It is wrong for people from different social classes to mix.

_____ (d) Trying to be heroic can have bad results.

19 Work with a partner. Decide which answer you think is best.

Why did Miles die?

(a) He was no longer possessed by Peter Quint.

(b) He had a weak heart.

(c) The governess killed him.

E Language

20 Underline the best form of the verbs in the sentences.

a. The governess often thought / was thinking about her employer.

b. One evening she saw / was seeing a man on top of the tower.

c. The sun went / was going down, so it was too dark to see his face clearly.

d. While she stared / was staring at him he disappeared.

21 Complete the extract from the story with the past simple or the past continuous of the verbs in brackets.

It (a) _____ (be) a gray, wet day, but there was enough light in the room for me to see my gloves on a chair near the window—and somebody outside! It was him! The man from the tower! I (b) _____ (gasp) with fear. He (c) _____ (stare) hard at my face for a few seconds and then he disappeared. I understood immediately that he (d) _____ (look for) somebody! But not me, somebody else.

22 Complete Mrs. Grose's questions about the man at the window. Use the verbs in the box in the correct form.

> do   look   recognize   see

a. Have you _____ him before?

b. Did you _____ him?

c. What was he _____ on the tower?

d. What does he _____ like?

23 Match the answers below to the questions in Exercise **22**.

——— ① No, he was a stranger.
——— ② He has curly red hair and a long pale face.
——— ③ Only standing and looking down at me.
——— ④ Yes, once. On the tower.

P **24** Complete the second sentence so that it means the same as the first. Use one or two words.

ⓐ The children's uncle sent them to live at Bly.
The children _____ to live at Bly by their uncle.

ⓑ Miles was a bit older than Flora.
Flora was a bit _____ Miles.

ⓒ They were easy children to look after.
They weren't _____ children to look after.

ⓓ The children had only a few toys.
The children didn't _____ toys.

25 Unscramble the letters and write the correct adjectives above the scrambled words

ⓐ The governess was completely PREESNIBLOS for the children.

ⓑ "Never, miss," she replied with a HARIMTPUNT smile.

ⓒ The children looked very sweet and TINONCNE.

ⓓ "I think you're RULEC!" Flora shouted at the governess.

ⓔ Was Miles sent away from school because he was DIWECK?

26 Find the noun forms of these verbs in the story.

ⓐ behave _____ ⓓ excite _____
ⓑ decide _____ ⓔ imagine _____
ⓒ disappoint _____ ⓕ suspect _____

TEST

56 1 Listen and tick (√) the correct picture.

a 1 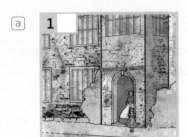   2

b 1    2

c 1    2

d 1    2

⭐ **2** Choose the correct answer 1, 2, 3 or 4.

_____ ⓐ Douglas knew the governess because _____.
　① he was her employer
　② he met her at university
　③ she worked for his family
　④ she belonged to his family

_____ ⓑ Mrs. Grose told the governess that Quint _____.
　① always dressed smartly
　② was often rude to her
　③ worked in the garden
　④ was put in charge of all the servants

_____ ⓒ During the night the governess saw the ghosts _____.
　① on the staircase
　② in the passage
　③ in her room
　④ on the lawn outside

_____ ⓓ Miles wanted to go back to school because _____.
　① he didn't like the governess
　② he wanted to be with boys of his age
　③ he was bored at Bly
　④ he liked studying

_____ ⓔ The governess told Mrs. Grose to take Flora away because _____.
　① she thought Mrs. Grose was in danger
　② she didn't like the child any more
　③ she wanted to be alone with Miles
　④ she wanted to continue teaching Miles

Famous Ghosts
in Books and Films

Work in small groups. Create an information poster on the following famous ghosts.

- *Sir Nicholas de Mimsy-Porpington*
- *Old King Hamlet*
- *The Ghost of Christmas Past*
- *Sir Simon de Canterville*
- *The Dead Men of Dunharrow*
- *Slimer*
- *The Headless Horseman*
- *The Flying Dutchman*

Before you start, find out:

- *the name of the book or film they appear in*
- *the author of the book or the director of the film*
- *what the ghosts do*

Illustrate your poster with pictures of the ghosts.

You can draw them or cut out pictures to stick on your poster.

Present your poster to the rest of the class.

作者簡介

亨利‧詹姆士（Henry James），1843年出生於紐約，家中五個孩子，他排行老二。他的雙親很富有，而且具有文化涵養。他在青少年期間，和家人旅居歐洲各地，長達數年。在這段期間，亨利進入私立學校就讀，也跟著私人家庭老師學習，學習多種語言，並飽覽許多歐洲著名作家的作品。

十九歲時，他在哈佛大學學法律，然而，他並未完成學業，因為他更沉浸於閱讀和寫作之中。 1864年，他出版了第一篇短篇故事，隨後便決心全心傾注於寫作上面。

1875年，他離開美國，旅居法國。隔年，搬到英國定居，於此終老。亨利‧詹姆士一生未娶，但他朋友很多，社交生活活躍。 1915年，第一次世界大戰開打，他成為英國公民。隔年二月，在倫敦辭世。

亨利‧詹姆士在一生中所創作的小說有二十餘部，其中最為人知的作品，包括《一位女士的畫像》（The Portrait of a Lady, 1881）、《波士頓人》（The Bostonians, 1886）、《奉使記》（The Ambassadors, 1903）和《金碗》（The Golden Bowl, 1904）。這些小說都改編過成電影，受到歡迎。他也寫了許多短篇故事和中篇小說（篇幅長度介於短篇小說和長篇小說之間），以及劇場的劇本、雜誌文章和旅遊書籍。

本書簡介

《碧廬冤孽》（The Turn of the Screw）出版於1898年，是亨利‧詹姆士最著名的鬼故事。19世紀末，鬼故事盛行，人們很著迷於超自然力量。

小說一開始先有一篇前言，介紹故事的主線。有一群朋友來到一間老舊的鄉村別墅，共度聖誕假期。這一天晚上，大家決定來講鬼故事，其中有一位說他讀過一個很恐怖的故事。當然，大家都興致勃勃地很想聽，他就請人把那個鬼故事的篇章，從倫敦的家裡寄過來。幾個夜晚之後，他就唸了這個故事給大家聽，而他講的這則故事，也就是這部中篇小說的主線。這個故事出自一位年輕的女家庭教師之手，內容是關於她的第一份工作。

她受雇於一位年輕英俊的男子，負責照顧年幼的姪子和姪女：十歲的邁爾斯和八歲的芙蘿拉。他們住在碧廬（Bly）鄉間的一座大房子裡，兩個孩子都長得漂亮又乖巧。女家庭教師抵達這座房子後不久，她看到了（或是自以為看到了）兩位已經過世的僕人的邪靈，分別是男僕昆特（Quint）和傑索小姐（Miss Jessel）。她確信兩個鬼魂可以跟孩子溝通，而且還打算傷害孩子。她決定，她一定要在事情發生之前，把自己的學生救出來。

是孩子們真的身陷危險之中，還是女家庭教師精神錯亂了？亨利‧詹姆士將結局留給讀者去決定。

楔子

P.15

平安夜時，我和幾個朋友待在鄉間的老宅邸。用過晚餐後，時間還早，我們點上蠟燭，圍坐在客廳的圍爐邊。

「這棟老房子讓我聯想到鬼故事。」葛瑞芬說。

「噢，那就說一個來聽聽吧！」女士們嚷嚷道。

「你們確定？可能會把你們嚇死了！」葛瑞芬問

大家都同意，這會兒需要的正是一點刺激，於是葛瑞芬便開始說起了故事。

故事講完的時候，大家動也不動，啞然無聲了好一會兒。這時，一位女士開口說道：「這故事真是詭異！一個看得到鬼的小孩，我還第一次聽過這樣的故事。」

過後，換了幾個人也講了故事，但是都很枯燥乏味。

我留意到，道格拉斯異常的安靜，我心想：「他有事想跟我們說。」

我猜想的果然沒有錯，就在大夥準備就寢之際，他開口說：「葛瑞芬的故事的確很詭異，但是，如果一個孩子就能夠造成那麼大的驚嚇，那要是故事換成兩個孩子的話呢？」

P.16

想當然耳，大家都興致勃勃地想聽這個故事。

「這個故事，我用講的講不出來，

我要用唸的，不過那篇故事放在倫敦的家中，鎖在抽屜裡。」道格拉斯說。

他看到大家一臉失望的表情，很快又說道：「如果可以，我明天一早就寫信給僕人，把抽屜的鑰匙寄給他，要他把故事寄過來。」

「道格拉斯，那故事是你寫的嗎？」我問。

他回答：「不是我寫的，是一位女性所寫的，她是我妹妹的家庭教師。二十多年前，她在過世之前，把這篇故事寄給了我。她是一位很有魅力的女性，比我大上十歲。我在某個暑假遇到她，我那時候還正在大學念書。我們常一塊去散步，我想我們是互相喜歡的。這件事情，她只跟我一個人說過。」

幾天後，這篇故事寄到了。傍晚，我們又聚集在客廳裡，大家都引頸期盼想聽這個故事。道格拉斯坐在壁爐邊的最

舒適的椅子上，故事的手稿就擱在他的
膝上。

他說道：「故事開始之前，我先說一下
故事的背景。這位女子是鄉下一名窮牧
師的么女，因為找工作，她決定去應徵
報上刊登的一個家庭教師職位。刊登者
回覆說，想要跟她見面，問她能否前來
倫敦一趟。

P. 18

「她立刻買了一張馬車車票，一個星期
之後，她踏上了旅程。刊登者在城裡的
高級住宅區，擁有一棟大宅邸。這時她
來到大門前，等候開門，心裡既興奮又
緊張。她當時只有二十歲，這是她應徵
的第一份工作。一位女侍應門，領她到
一個小房間內等候。

「幾分鐘後，房子的主人過來迎接
她。主人的外表，出乎她的意料之外，
年輕、英俊，而且很會穿著，就像言情
小說中的男主角，或者說，是鄉間窮牧
師的女兒的夢中情人！她猜想，他也一
定很有錢，因為房子裡擺滿了漂亮的物
品。他在她對面的位子坐下，說明情況。

『我在幫我的小姪子和姪女找家庭教
師。』他帶著笑容對她說。

『他們的父母，也就是我的弟弟和弟
媳，他們兩年前在印度過世了，孩子們
如今在這個世上無依無靠，我想幫助可
憐的孩子們，不過我還沒有結婚，不知
道怎麼帶小孩。我把他們送到碧廬，那
是我位於艾賽克斯郡的房子。鄉間比城
市安全多了，空氣也較清新，你不這麼
認為嗎？』

年輕女子點了點頭。莫名地，她就是

很想幫助他，他實在非常迷人。

P. 19

他繼續說道：『葛洛斯太太是碧廬的
女管家，她很能幹，帶領很多僕人。孩
子們的第一位女家庭教師，很不幸地突
然去世。她是一位很和善的年輕女子，
孩子們很喜愛她。之後，我們送邁爾斯
去學校念書，葛洛斯太太負責照顧芙蘿
拉。你將負責照顧芙蘿拉，在邁爾斯回
家度假時，你就負責照顧他們兩個人。』」

房子的主人

• 房子的主人是什麼樣的人？
• 他喜愛孩子嗎？
• 年輕女主角喜歡他嗎？
• 他準備錄用她嗎？和朋友一起討論。

「他給她薪資很優渥，但是她不確定是

否想接受這份工作。待在鄉間，只有兩個孩子可以作伴，她怕會很孤單。」

「不過，她還是接下了這份工作。」我說。

「是的，她接受了。」道格拉斯回答。

「因為她愛上了男主人。」

「她只見過他兩次。」

「要墜入情網，只需要一會兒的時間。」我回答。

P. 20

道格拉斯站起身，翻動壁爐內的柴火。

「你說的對。」他一邊說，一邊望著熊熊燃燒的柴火，「愛情真是難以捉摸，可不是？她明明知道自己不會再見到他，卻還是接受了這份工作。」

「她怎麼會知道？」

「這是這份工作開出的條件之一，而且還是最重要的條件。他說：『如果你接受這份工作，你就負責照顧孩子們，料理他們的一切。然後，你不能寫信給我，也不能跟我聯繫。我什麼事情都不想知道。你同意我的條件嗎？』

『我同意。』她回答。」

「這篇故事的名稱是什麼，道格拉斯？」席間有人默默地問道。

「沒有名稱。」他說完後，坐了下來。接著，他翻開手稿已經褪色的紅色封頁，開始唸起故事。

第一章　碧廬

P. 21

在艾賽克斯郡的驛站，已經有一輛馬車在那裡等我。

這是一個宜人的六月傍晚，在前往碧廬的一路上，我享受著鄉間的美麗風景。

別墅建築很令人喜歡，不是我想像中的那種陰鬱的地方。屋前有一片草坪，種了很多花。鳥兒在枝頭盤旋，徜徉在無雲的藍天中。我對這份工作的疑慮也一掃而空，「你做了正確的決定，你待在這裡會很快樂。」我告訴自己。

女管家和小女孩，她們出現在門口來迎接我。我立刻發現，小女孩長得非常漂亮，有一頭金色的捲髮、一雙湛藍的眼睛，小臉蛋洋溢著甜美的笑容，讓我聯想到了義大利古畫中的天使。

「小姐，您經過一番舟車勞頓，一定很渴了吧？快進來，喝杯茶！」葛洛斯太太面帶笑容說道。

她領我到餐廳去，在接下來的一個鐘頭裡，我們相談甚歡。她是一個和藹可親的婦女，我很快就喜歡她這個人，我想：「我們一定可以成為好朋友。」

喝過茶之後，她帶我到我的房間。我的房間位於房子的前端，所以從窗戶望去，可以看到花園的美麗景緻。

P. 23

「這棟房子裡，這是最好的房間了。」她對我說。

「房間又漂亮又寬敞！」我說。

在房間的另一頭，有一張較小的床。

「那一定是要給芙蘿拉睡的床。」我說。

「是的，小姐。但是我跟她說了，她今天晚上可以跟我睡，希望你不要介意，她跟你還不熟，可能會怕跟陌生人睡在同一個房間裡。這樣可以嗎？」葛洛斯太太說。

「謝謝你，葛洛斯太太，你想的很周到。」我回答。

看到女管家對小女孩明顯的關愛，我更喜愛女管家這個人了。

當天稍晚，在用晚餐的時候，我向她問起了芙蘿拉的哥哥。

「他是不是也長得像天使一樣？」我問。

「是的，小姐！」她帶著笑容回答：「他長得跟芙蘿拉一樣漂亮！」

「他明天就會返家，是不是？」

「不是明天，小姐，是星期五。」

「我可以到馬車站去接他，芙蘿拉也可以一道去，他會喜歡這樣吧，葛洛斯太太？」我說。

「是啊，這聽起來不錯。」她說。

我很高興我們對於每一件事情都能夠有共識。我想，她之所以尊重我，是因為我是家庭教師，她似乎也非常開心我能夠來到這裡。

P. 24

當天晚上，我興奮得睡不著覺，我不敢相信自己的運氣這麼好。芙蘿拉好漂亮、好迷人，而且也是一個聰明伶俐的小女孩。我想：「教導她功課，一定是令人愉快。」

最後，我終於睡去了，但是夜裡醒來了幾次，每一次，我的眼前都浮現出芙蘿拉美麗的小臉蛋。有一度，我還以為房間外傳來了孩子的哭聲，還有輕聲的腳步聲。

「真蠢，你不過是在作夢，快睡吧！」我這樣跟自己說。

隔天早晨，我決定請我的學生帶我去逛一趟花園和宅邸。如果立刻就要開始上課，會讓我感到焦慮。碧廬這地方令我感到有些害怕，這裡跟我的家鄉很不一樣。何況，我想這也是一個可以讓我更加認識芙蘿拉的好方法。

她對於我的提議感到很高興，早餐一吃完，我們立刻開始去逛花園。她帶我去看每一個角落、每一棵樹木和每一朵花。我們一直聊得很開心，半個鐘頭之後，我們就成了好朋友。

她的年紀雖小，但並不羞怯。她對自己很有自信，什麼都不怕。房子裡，每一個陰暗的角落、每一個空蕩的房間，她都敢走進去。她跑狹窄的階梯，站在塔頂。她一襲藍色的洋裝，搭配一頭金色的捲髮，讓我聯想起小精靈的模樣。

P. 25

那天晚上，晚餐過後，一個女僕交給我一封信。我打開信箋，看到裡面有雇主寫給我的短箋，並挾帶了另外一封信函。

信函上寫道：

這封信件，是邁爾斯學校的校長寫來的，他是一個無趣的人。請你讀他的來信，由你全權處理。請勿聯繫我，我將遠行。

P. 26

我把校長的來信帶回房間，在就寢前閱讀。看過之後，我覺得很難過，信的內容讓我第二晚又失眠了。隔天早晨醒來，我感到疲憊又不安，不知道該拿這封信如何是好。最後，我決定把信拿給葛洛斯太太看。

「退學！」我把校長的信唸給她聽之後，她跟著重複這個字眼，「我不懂，校長這這話是什麼意思？男孩不都是……？」

我回答：「送回家？對，沒錯，不過他們都只是回家度假，但是，退學是指邁爾斯以後都不能再回學校了！校長不希望他回學校，他說，邁爾斯不應該跟其他的孩子在一起。」

學校

• 下列的名詞描述的是英國不同種類的學校，用這些字各造一個句子。可以參考字典。
boarding 寄宿學校
mixed 男女混合公立中學
secondary 中等學校
public 英國公學
nursery 幼稚園
comprehensive 綜合學校

「邁爾斯主人！」女管家氣憤地說道：「他們怎麼能說出這樣殘酷的話？他也才十歲啊！」

「真令人難以置信。」我說。

女管家改變了神情，她很高興我認同她的說法。

P. 27

「他在家裡會調皮嗎？」我問。

「他是個男孩，小姐，男孩都有頑皮的時候。」她帶著笑容回答：「你先見過之後，再看他是不是很調皮。」

隔天，芙蘿拉跟我準備前往馬車驛站，去接邁爾斯。在等候馬車來接的時候，我跟葛洛斯太太問起了前一任家庭教師的事。

「她長得什麼樣子？」

「她很年輕、很漂亮，差不多就像你一樣！」她回答。

「她是在這裡過世的嗎？」

「不是，小姐，她當時已經離開。」

「你是説她生了病，然後回家過世的？」

「也不是，她在這裡的時候並未染病。她是在年底離開碧廬，回家過短暫的假期，但就沒有再回來了。後來，主人跟我們説，她過世了。」

「她是怎麼過世的？」

「小姐，主人沒有告訴我。小姐，如果你不介意，我得回去工作了。」葛洛斯太太説。

第二章　窗戶上的臉龐

P. 29

邁爾斯正在馬車站等候我們。葛洛斯太太説得沒錯，他長得跟妹妹一樣漂亮，甚至還來得更俊俏。他的一雙藍眼眸，透出無邪的眼神，我從未見過哪個孩子像他這樣。在返回碧廬的途中，我的心整個都在他的身上。

我趁著空檔的時間，去找葛洛斯太太。

「校長的那封信真是太蠢了！你有看過比邁爾斯還要貼心的孩子嗎？」我説。

「我也沒看過，小姐。」她的臉上帶著勝利的笑容，她很高興我跟她一樣喜歡邁爾斯，「那麼，你打算怎麼回應那封信，小姐？」

「我什麼也不做！我不會寫信給他的伯父，也不會對邁爾斯透露任何事。」我回答。

她握住我的手好一會兒，然後説：「我支持你，小姐。」

我很感謝她，便雙手抱住她，在她的臉頰上吻了一下。

接下來的幾個星期，日子過得很愉快。白天，我忙著照顧孩子，但是等他們都上床睡覺了，我有一個鐘頭的時間屬於自己，這也是我一天當中最喜歡的時刻。夏夜漫漫，所以我都會到花園裡去走走。

P. 30

漫步在天色漸自暗了的夜裡，我常常會想起雇主。我遵照他的囑咐去做，做得也很好，我對自己感到很滿意。我想像著會在花園的小徑上遇見他，想像著見到他的臉龐、他的笑容，表達對我的讚許。

一天晚上，當我又在花園小徑上漫步時，發生了一件奇怪的事。我像往常一樣想著我的雇主，他英俊的臉龐，清晰地浮現在我的腦海裡，就在這時，突然間我看到了他！他並非站在我面前的花園小徑上，而是站在遠處的高塔上。

我兩度屏住呼吸，一開始是驚訝，接著感到震驚。但是，不，那不是他！那是別的男人！我們對視了幾分鐘，我想要跟他說話，但是他離我離得很遠。接著，他移步走向塔的另外一邊，但眼睛始終盯著我不放，最後消失無蹤。

我感到害怕、困惑和惱怒，他是誰？他在那裡做什麼？碧廬是否藏著什麼「祕密」？

我又走了一會兒，回到房間後，我的心情鎮定了一些。

「他大概只是一個好奇的遊客，想要看看夜幕逐漸低垂的花園和宅邸。重要的是，反正他現在已經走了。」我對自己說。

我想把那名男子拋在腦後，專注在工作上，而這並不難，因為我樂在工作中。邁爾斯和芙蘿拉佔滿我白天的時間，帶給我歡樂。

P. 32

他們倆真是十分可愛的孩子。邁爾斯是個格外敏感的孩子，他沒說過學校的事，我也不過問。不過，我更加確定，是校長搞錯了。這孩子很單純，不會做出什麼壞事，而對敏感的孩子來說，學校是個殘酷的地方。

幾天後，我又看見了那個男人。當時是星期天的午後，葛洛斯太太和我正準備去上教堂。我到處找不到我的手套，然後我記起來手套應該是在餐廳。我快步走下樓，去找手套，因為我不想要遲到。我打開餐廳的門，環顧四周。當天的天氣濕冷陰暗，但室內光線足以讓我看到手套就擱在窗邊的椅子上，而且還看到有人在外頭！是他！那個塔頂的男人。

我一陣心驚。他盯著我的臉看了一會兒，然後消失不見。我立刻明白了，他是在找人！但是他不是要找我，他要找的是別人。頓時，我就對他不再感到害怕了。

我奔出房子，衝進花園，但是花園裡沒有人。我環顧四周，確定男子並未躲在林間或樹叢裡。我不知道他怎麼不見了。

接著，我把臉貼近窗戶的玻璃，往餐廳望了望，我看見葛洛斯太太站在門邊。她一看到我，立刻轉身衝了出來。不一會兒，她來到我的身邊。

P. 33

「怎麼回事？你的臉色怎麼那麼白！你的氣色很難看！」她大喊道。

白得像紙
• 用你自己的想法，用以下明喻／比喻的話來造句，並在班上分享你的想法。
  黑得像……
  勇敢得像……
  冷得像……
  餓得像……

「我看見窗戶外有一個男人，我很怕。」我說。

「現在他人呢？」她問。

「我不知道。」我回答。

「你之前見過他嗎？」

「有見過一次，在塔頂。」

「你認識他嗎？」

「不認識，他是一個陌生人。」

「他站在塔頂做什麼？」

「只是站在那裡，往下看著我。」

「你怎麼沒跟我說呢，他是一名紳士嗎？」

我不加思索地回答：「不是，他不是紳士，他是個鬼魂！」

P. 34

「鬼魂！這是什麼意思？」她說。

我看到她也受到了驚嚇。她迅速轉身，望向花園，不過這時候天色已經太暗，什麼都看不到了。

接著，她突然說：「現在該去教堂了。」

「我不去教堂了，我不能把孩子們獨自留下。」我回答。

「難道你怕……？」葛洛斯太太不願把心裡所想的字眼說出來。

「怕他會再回來？」我說：「是的，我怕。」

管家沒有再多說些什麼，只是一臉焦慮。

「她知道這個男人的事。」我心想。

過了一會兒，她才問：「他長得什麼樣子？」

「他有一頭紅色的捲髮，臉長長的，很蒼白，眼睛很小，目光很奇怪。他看起來像個演員，你知道的，高高挺挺的樣子。不過，他絕不會是什麼紳士，噢，不！不會是紳士！」我回答。

「他的穿著呢？」

「穿著體面，但是衣服顯然不是他的。」

她雙手緊握，目光望向別處。「他穿的是主人的衣服！」她說。

「這麼說，你認識他？」

她沒有立刻回答，接著才喊出：「昆特！」

「昆特？」

P. 35

「彼得‧昆特，他是主人的僕人，他們去年都還一起待在這裡。主人的一些衣服不見了，我懷疑是昆特拿去了，但主人沒說什麼。後來，主人便離家了，而昆特留了下來。」葛洛斯太太解釋道。

「自己留了下來？」

「對，留下來和我們在一起。」她低頭望著雙手，「他負責照顧我們。」

「他發生了什麼事？」

沉默了好一會兒之後，她才說：「他也走了。」

「走去哪裡了？」

她驚訝地看著我，說道：「我不知道。」

後來，停頓好一陣子之後，她又說：「他死了。」

「死了？」我幾乎尖叫出聲。

「是的，昆特先生死了！」

第三章　湖邊的女子

P. 36

由於前往教堂的時間太晚了，於是葛洛斯太太跟我返回屋內，在教室內繼續我們的談話。

「你說他在找人。」管家說。

「他在找邁爾斯，他要找的人是邁爾斯。」我回答。

「但你怎麼知道？」

「我就是知道！」我大聲驚呼道：「你也知道，葛洛斯太太，我們要保護孩子們！你會幫我吧？」

這位善良的女人點頭同意。她相信我跟她的事，她並不覺得我發瘋了。

「奇怪的是，孩子們不曾談起他。」我說。

「芙蘿拉大概不記得他，但是邁爾斯跟昆特常在一起相處，他們是『很要好的朋友』，這是昆特自己說的。昆特對邁爾斯予取予求，他對每個人都予取予求。」她說。

「這麼說，他是個壞人。」我說。

「我知道他是個壞人，但是主人並不這麼認為。」她回答。

「你為什麼沒有告訴他？」

「他怕麻煩，不想知道。總之，他很信任昆特，所以他才要昆特照顧我們，包括孩子們。」她說。

「真是可怕！」我大喊道。

P. 37

「是啊。」她說完後，流下了眼淚。

那天夜裡，我無法入睡，我不斷想著昆特這個人。我確信葛洛斯太太知道他的許多事，但是她不願意告訴我。

隔天，我們碰面時，我要她多說一些他的事。

「主人離家後，他在碧廬待了幾個月。後來，一個冬天的清晨，在往村子的路上，他的屍體被人發現了，他像是在結冰的地面上摔倒了，碰撞到頭部。有人說，他當時喝醉了。」她說。

「你相信這個說法嗎？」我問。

「彼得・昆特是個壞人，他有很多惡習，他的過去有很多不為人知的祕密，我們無法確定他的死因。」她說。

這時，我瞭解到，我的工作比我所想的還要困難。孩子們在這世上無依無靠，他們身陷危險之中，而我是唯一能夠保護他們的人，我得像英雄般地勇敢面對！我一點都不擔心，這是我的大好機會，可以讓我贏得雇主的敬重。

我開始花更多時間陪伴孩子。我在等待著事情發生，有時候，這種懸疑感壓得我有點喘不過氣來，我都覺得我快瘋了。終於，在一天的午後，事情爆發了。

P. 38

我跟芙蘿拉正在花園裡，那天，太陽很大，我和年輕的學生待在湖邊的樹蔭下。我們玩著芙蘿拉想出來的遊戲。這是這兩個孩子都很擅長的事，我從來不必想點子來讓他們開心。

這座湖叫做阿左夫海（這是我們在地理課上想出來的），我們都扮演著芙蘿拉故事中的角色。

當時，她正自顧自地說著話，我在一旁做著女紅，突然，我感到還有其他人在場。我抬起眼，看見阿左夫海的對岸出現了一個人！那是一個女人，我可以清楚看見她的模樣。

她站在蘆葦叢間，望著我們。起初，我以為她是家中的僕人，或是村子裡的人。在碧廬，遇到兜售東西的生意人，並非罕事。我望著芙蘿拉，我們相離的並不遠。

「她一定認得對方，她可以告訴我那個人是誰。」我心想。

我屏住呼吸，等她認出對方之後，再發出驚呼。然而，什麼事也沒發生。之後，最令人感到毛骨悚然的是，她轉身背對著湖，繼續靜靜地玩著她的遊戲。我看著她，她正專注地用一片木頭和一根樹枝在造一艘小船。

P. 40

等我返回宅邸之後，我立刻去找葛洛斯太太。

「他們知道！」我抱著她，大聲喊道：「太可怕了，他們知道！他們知道！」

「你在說什麼？」她說道，很驚訝看到我這麼激動。

「我們所知道的事！也許還超乎我們所知道的！」

我將身體拉開，努力保持冷靜。

「兩個鐘頭前，在花園！」我解釋說：「芙蘿拉看見了！」

「她有跟你說，她看到了？」管家焦急地問道。

「沒有，她沒說什麼，你想想！一個八歲的孩子！」

我還是覺得無法置信。

家庭教師

• 為什麼家庭教師這麼苦惱？
• 她很難相信什麼事？
• 她知道蘆葦叢間的那個女人是誰嗎？

「那你又是怎麼知道？」葛洛斯太太問。

「我當時也在那裡！我親眼看著她的，芙蘿拉知情！」

「你是説她看見了他？」

「不是他！」我説：「是她！」

我的話嚇到了管家。

P. 41

我繼續往下説：「是另外一個人，一個全身穿著黑衣服的女人，一個可怕的邪靈！她站在湖的另一頭。」

「你認得她嗎？」

「我不認得，但是芙蘿拉認得。你也見過她，葛洛斯太太，她是前任家庭教師！」

「傑索小姐？」

「是的，傑索小姐！」我驚呼道：「她盯著芙蘿拉看，噢！她的眼神很可怕！」

葛洛斯太太未發一語，等著我繼續往下説。

「她想要芙蘿拉！我看她的眼神就知道了，芙蘿拉也知道！」我大喊。

管家面色蒼白，轉身走近窗邊。「你説她全身穿著黑衣服。」她靜靜説著。

「是的，而且她很漂亮，非常漂亮，但是看起來很邪惡！」我説。

葛洛斯太太緩緩走向我。

「是的，傑索小姐很邪惡！」她説完，就緊緊地握住我的手，「跟昆特一樣，他們都很邪惡。」

「現在，你一定要把他們兩個人的事都跟我説，葛洛斯太太。他們之間有什麼關係？是情侶關係嗎？」

「是的，他們是情侶。」

「儘管他只是一個……」

P. 42

「……只是一個僕人，而她是一位淑女？是的。」接著，她激動地説道：「但是他才不在乎，他目中無人。」

「真是一個可怕的男人！」

「最後，她只得離開，不能留在這裡。」

「葛洛斯太太，她的死因是什麼？」

「我不知道，也不想知道。」她説。

半晌之後，她緩緩地説：「但我會去想像，我到現在還是會去想。但是我的想像很可怕，説不出口。」

一聽到這裡，我哭了出來。

「我想要救孩子們！」我啜泣地説：「但是太遲了！他們已經迷失了！」

第四章　壞男孩

P. 43

那天深夜，葛洛斯太太進來我的房間，我們又聊了很久。她認同我的話，覺得那些鬼魂一定是真的，因為我對昆特和傑索小姐的描述很符合。現在，我們兩個最擔心的是孩子們。孩子們知道了什麼？是不是對我們有所隱瞞？

「我不相信他們是壞孩子，他們跟我在一起時很乖巧。」我説。

接著，我記起讀完校長的信之後，葛洛斯太太説過的話：「男孩都有頑皮的時候。」我提起這句話來詢問她。

我問：「你説的這句話是什麼意思？跟我説吧，親愛的管家，我要知道一切來龍去脈。」

她猶豫了一會兒，我耐心等著她回答。

終於，她開口説：「這個嘛，有幾個月的時間，邁爾斯都和昆特待在一起。在我看來，他們相處太多了。我提醒傑索小姐要注意，但是她不以為意。有一天，我對邁爾斯談了這件事，我試著跟他解釋説，一位紳士不應該花太多時間和僕人待在一起，但是……」

她突然一陣臉紅，將目光移開。我替她把話説完。

P. 44

「……但是，他説你也是僕人。」

「是的，而且他還否認有些下午並沒有跟昆特在一起，但是我知道他們都在一起。」

「所以他跟你撒謊，」我説：「這一點都不像邁爾斯。」

接下來的幾天，我時時刻刻看顧著孩子，他們會不會覺得很奇怪？他們是否明白我只想要保護他們，不讓他們被邪惡的昆特和傑索小姐所控制？

我盡量不在他們的面前顯露出我的恐懼，但我有時候會忍不住雙手緊緊環抱住他們。這段期間，他們變得很喜歡我，總是做些什麼來逗我開心。他們讀書也更用功了，並為了我學寫詩、編故事。他們唱歌，邁爾斯也會彈奏新的鋼琴曲目。在課堂上，沒有一刻是沉悶的。

兩個孩子都很聰明，尤其是邁爾斯，他學習東西特別快。他很擅長閱讀，可以自己從書本上學習到很多東西，我根本不用擔心要為他找另外一間學校。我寧可選擇遺忘，這是我的毛病。總之，對他來説，我不認為學校會是最好的地方。他可以和芙蘿拉待在碧廬，這才是更好的。兄妹倆在一起很快樂，他們從不吵架，而且什麼祕密都會跟對方説。

P. 45

自學

• 和朋友談談在家自學的事。（在父母或是家庭教師的指導下，在家念書。）
• 孩子們為什麼有時候需要在家自學？
• 在家自學，各有什麼優缺點？
• 你喜歡在家自學還是去學校上課？

日子就這樣過去了。我沒有太多自己的時間，但是當我空閒下來時，我就會看些書。碧廬有很多藏書，我的房間裡都會放本書。

這天晚上，我由於太過沉浸於書中的情節，沒有注意到時間。等到我把書本闔上時，時間已經很晚了。就在這時候，房間的門外傳來了聲響，有人在屋子裡走動。我把書本放下，拿起蠟燭，來到走廊上，靜靜地把身後的房門鎖上。

我把燭台舉高，沿著走廊，來到樓梯口的大窗戶前面。

就在這時候，同時間發生了三件事情。我的蠟燭熄滅了，我注意到外面的天色微亮，而且我聽到有人正走上樓梯。窗戶照進微弱的光線，我看清楚了樓梯上的人影，那是昆特！他樓梯正走到一半！

P.46

當他看到我的時候，他停下腳步，我們對視著。我們離得很近，但是都一語未發。這就像在半夜裡，正當全屋子的人都睡著的時候，撞見了闖進門的小偷一樣。他看起來就像一個活生生的人，反倒是我們之間的沉默才顯得非自然。幸好，我並不感到害怕，而他也知道。我們站在那裡，彼此對看了好一陣子。之後，他轉過身去，走下樓梯，消失在黑暗之中。

等我確定他已經離開之後，我沿著走廊，回到我的房間。我靜靜地打開房門的鎖，走進房間。

最後映入我的眼裡的是，芙蘿拉的床是空的。我的心跳幾乎要停止，她去哪裡了？接著，我聽到窗戶那邊有聲響，而她就站在窗簾的後面。

「你這個壞家庭教師！」在我還未開口

之前，她先說道：「你去哪裡了？」

我並沒有生她的氣，反而是鬆了一口氣。我在我的椅子上坐了下來，她立刻朝著我跑過來，在我的腿上坐下。她穿著睡衣，臉頰紅通通的，一頭金色的捲髮，看上去就是一個小天使。

「你為什麼望著窗外？你以為我在花園裡，是嗎？」我問。

「我起床，是因為我覺得窗戶外面有人。」她很正經地回答。

P.48

「那你有看到誰了嗎？」

她猶豫了一會兒，回答：「沒有。」

不知怎麼的，我立刻覺得她在撒謊，大概是因為我太緊張了。我想說：「你看見誰了？跟我說實話！你知道我是知情的，對不對！」

但是我沒開口說這些。我站起身，說道：「你為什麼要把窗簾拉到床邊？要讓我以為你人還在？」

她給我一個最甜美的微笑說：「因為我不想嚇到你。」

在這之後，我每天晚上都很晚才闔眼。等到我確定芙蘿拉睡著了，我才靜靜地離開房間。我走到樓梯口，但是我沒有再見到昆特。倒是有一回，我在樓梯口看見傑索小姐。她就坐在樓梯底，雙手摀著臉，我想她是在掩面哭泣，然後，她沒有轉身，突然就消失無蹤。

鬼魂

- 和朋友一起討論什麼是鬼魂？
- 他們會傷害人嗎？
- 每個人都能看見他們嗎？

P. 50

第十一天晚上，我決定早一點上床睡覺，因為我實在是太疲倦了。我立刻倒頭睡著，但是在凌晨一點時，醒了過來。這時房間內沒有絲毫光線，我第一個想法是，「芙蘿拉把蠟燭吹熄了」。

我跳下床，把蠟燭再點亮。芙蘿拉沒有躺在床上，她站在窗邊，望著夜色。她沒有注意到我已經醒來，所以我很確定她正看著什麼東西或什麼人，就在下方的花園那裡。

「一定是傑索小姐。」我心想。

我悄悄地打開房門，來到走廊。我想知道芙蘿拉究竟在看什麼，我得找到另一扇可以觀看花園視野的窗戶。我在邁爾斯的門外聆聽了一會兒，並沒有聽到什麼聲響。於是我趕往塔頂的空房間，打開窗戶，望向下方的草坪。我看到一個人正望向我這邊，但並不是在看我，而是望向我的上方。

「樓上窗口邊一定有人。」我心想。月亮的光線足以讓我看清楚花園裡的人，我認出了那個人，我感到一陣不安。那個人正是可憐的小邁爾斯！

第五章　危險的朋友

P. 51

我並沒有叫住邁爾斯，因為我不想把屋子裡的人都吵醒。我快步走下樓，來到花園。他看到我的時候，一語不發，他只是走向我，讓我帶他回屋子裡。

等我帶著他回房間後，我把手搭在他的肩膀上，嚴肅地盯著他看。

「邁爾斯，你現在一定要跟我說實話，你為什麼跑到外面去？」

他對著我微笑，那一刻在月光的照耀之下，他看上去就像是一個精靈小王子。

「如果我告訴你原因，你會明白嗎？」
我點點頭。

他溫柔地說：「嗯，我是要讓你知道，我有時候也會是一個調皮的男孩！」

接著，他走上前來，給我一個親吻。他的回答和親吻，都讓我很吃驚，我幾乎要哭出來。我雙手環抱住他，回吻他。我無法言語。

「我上床睡覺時，沒有換衣服。」他一邊解釋，一邊掙開我的手，「我坐在床上看書，看到半夜，然後走下樓。你看，當我使壞時，我是真的很壞！」

P.52

「你是如何計畫讓我驚醒的？」我問。

「我告訴芙蘿拉，要她起床，望向窗外。」他還是用很溫柔的聲音繼續說道：「她發出的聲音把你吵醒了，你想知道她在看什麼，你就也看了看，然後就看到我了。」

「夜裡會著涼！」我說道，想發脾氣一下。

他笑了笑，回答說：「是啊，我很壞，對不對？」

我看得出來，他感到很自豪。我不知道該怎麼跟他說，就再親吻了他一次，然後走出房間。

P.53

一直到隔天晚上，我才有機會跟葛洛斯太太談。我很高興能夠跟她分享我的煩惱和祕密，只要跟她聊一聊，我就感覺好很多。我跟她說什麼，她都會很有耐心地聽我講。她自己不會去多想，她只看到孩子們是這麼漂亮、貼心和聰明。

陽光還很暖和，我邀請她跟我在花園裡坐一會兒。孩子們在我們面前不遠處的草坪上嬉戲，邁爾斯正在讀故事給芙蘿拉聽。葛洛斯太太一邊盯著他們看，一邊聽我說話，臉上掛著愉快的笑容。

我開始向她描述夜裡發生的事，但她不是很有興致。她似乎並不明白事情的嚴重性。

「邁爾斯最後跟我說的時候，說出了實話。」當我說到這裡時，她才豎起耳朵。

「是什麼？」她問。

「『你不知道我會有多壞！』」我帶著勝利的表情，看著管家說：「邁爾斯清楚知道自己可以表現得很壞，這是當然的。學校的校長也知道這一點。」

「但是你說校長的封信太蠢了！」葛洛斯太太略帶慍怒地說道：「你對孩子們的看法有了改變？」

「不，沒有，我只是開始弄清楚碧廬究竟發生了什麼事。」我回答。

「究竟發生了什麼事？」

P. 54

「我很確定他們四個人，邁爾斯、芙蘿拉、傑索小姐和昆特，他們經常碰面。看看現在的孩子們，看起來那麼天真可愛，不是嗎？但是，他們一直都把我們蒙在鼓裡。邁爾斯並不是在唸童話故事給芙蘿拉聽，而是在跟她講他們的事！那兩個鬼魂！」

孩子們正在草坪間嬉戲，葛洛斯太太臉上的表情，透露出她很難相信我所說的話。

我繼續往下說：「我第一次見到孩子們的時候，就覺得他們很特別，之前我說不出原因，但我現在明白了。這兩個孩子跟一般的孩子不同，他們長得太漂亮、太乖巧，但是卻一直在欺騙我們。他們不過是在玩一個遊戲，他們並不是乖巧，而是心神不在這裡。」

葛洛斯太太沒有說任何話，只是瞪著我看。

你是怎麼看的？

•葛洛斯太太相信家庭教師的話嗎？
•如果邁爾斯和芙蘿拉在玩一場遊戲，他們為什麼要這麼做？
•「一般的孩子」是什麼樣子的？和同學分享看法。

P. 56

「我知道這聽起來很瘋狂，但這是千真萬確的。他們不屬於我們，不屬於我，不屬於我們。他們是他和她的！」我回答。

「昆特跟那女人的？」

「是的！他們想要占有孩子。」

這對葛洛斯太太來說，幾乎很難接受。

「但為什麼呢？」她一邊問，一邊轉身望向孩子們：「他們為什麼要擁有這些可憐的小東西？」

「因為他們想透過孩子，繼續他們的邪惡力量！」

「邪惡力量！」葛洛斯太太臉色發白，「什麼邪惡力量？」

「過去幾個月，他們和孩子們相處時，他們在孩子身上灌輸邪惡的想法。他們想要繼續他們的邪惡力量，因為這可以把他們帶回到這個世界。」我解釋說。

「噢，老天！真是太惡毒了！」葛洛斯太太驚呼道：「但他們現在打算怎麼做？」

「怎麼做？」我幾乎是用喊的。

孩子們聽到我的聲音，停了下來。他們朝我們微笑、揮手，繼續嬉戲。

「他們會毀了孩子們！他們還不知道要怎麼做，但他們會想出辦法。他們那

110

一刻在奇怪的地方出沒，在塔頂、在湖的另一邊、在窗戶外，他們很快就會得逞，而且……」

「……而且孩子們會跟他們走……」葛洛斯太太低聲說。

「……而且還會因此賠上性命！」

P. 57

葛洛斯太太站起身，走離開我一段距離。

「所以在孩子受到傷害之前，我們一定要阻止他們。」我說。

我的朋友沉默良久。她佇立著，望向花園，我知道她正在想辦法。

最後她開口說：「他們的伯父一定得出來阻止這件事，他一定要把孩子們帶走。」

「那誰要去跟他講？」我問。

她轉過身來，望著我：「你來說，小姐。」

「但是他要我不管發生什麼事，都不可以跟他聯絡。」

葛洛斯太太的目光望著孩子們好一會兒，然後回到椅子上坐下。她抓住我的手臂說：「你一定得讓他過來一趟，他得回來這裡，幫幫我們。」

我們望著彼此，她看出我的心思。

「如果由我來寫信，他會嘲笑我，也不會再尊重我，他會覺得我不過是想要吸引他的注意。」

女人之間可以互相懂得這種事。

「我不能夠寫信給他，如果你寫信給他，洩漏了這件事……」我說。

她這下子可是怕我了。

「……我就會立刻離開碧廬。」

第六章　艱難的決定

P. 58

幾個星期過去，夏季結束了。進入初秋，天氣開始變化。天空每天都灰濛濛的，又濕又冷。那幾個星期裡，我常想到要跟孩子們問昆特和傑索小姐的事，但始終提不起勇氣。

一個星期日上午，在我們前往教堂的路上，邁爾斯突然問我，「我什麼時候可以回學校？」

他的問題讓我很詫異，我還不知道要怎麼回答他。

他看到我一臉困惑，便繼續往下說：「你知道的，男孩不能老是跟小姐混在一起，這不太好。當然，你是一個很好的小姐，但我是一個男孩，我愈來愈大了。」

「是啊，你的確愈來愈大了。」我最後擠出話來。

「所以，我什麼時候可以回學校？」

「你在學校快樂嗎？」我問。

「我在任何地方都很快樂。」

「既然這樣，那就留在碧廬吧！」

「但是我想要看更多的東西，而且我想要跟同齡的男孩在一起。」他補充說道。

我們就要走到教堂，而葛洛斯太太和芙蘿拉已經進入了教堂內。

P. 59

就在我們快到教堂的門口時，邁爾斯問：「伯父知道我已經長大了嗎？」

「我想他可能不是很清楚。」

「這麼說，他不會來了。」

「到碧廬？誰能讓他來呢？」我問。

「我！我會讓他來！」邁爾斯說完，便跑進教堂裡。

我並沒有跟進去，因為我很激動。我在教堂外的庭園徘徊，想著剛才的對話。現在事情很清楚了，邁爾斯已經有所打算。他知道，我不敢要求他的伯父前來碧廬，所以他想要利用我的恐懼，來達到他的目的：他想回學校。

我突然怕起他來了。我想要離開碧廬，忘掉這一切。有個聲音在我的腦海裡說：「現在就走！趁大家都在教堂時，快回去打包行李吧！」

我猶豫著，我這麼做好嗎？我要趕快做出決定。

「好，離開吧。」我心想。

我快步走過教堂的庭園和花園。

當我回到靜悄悄的房子裡時，一想到自己就要離開，我開始覺得很興奮。

「如果你的動作夠快，就可以走得無聲無息，但是動作得夠快才行！」我對自己說。

然而，當我對自己的逃離再想得仔細些之後，興奮之情立刻轉為絕望。要去驛站，還有一段距離，沒有馬車，我怎麼去呢？

P. 61

我在樓梯上坐了下來，用手搗著臉，這時我想起了傑索小姐。一個月前，我就是在我現在坐的地方，看到她用手搗住臉的！這個畫面令我感到害怕。我很快站起身，上樓走到教室裡，收拾我的東西。

我卻吃驚地看到有個女人就坐在我的

桌前，她正用我的筆在寫信。起初，我以為她是一名僕人。接著，她站起身，在屋內走動。我認出那一身黑色的衣裳、美麗的臉龐和憂傷的神情，那是傑索小姐！

「你這個惡毒、可憐的女人！」我對她發出咆哮。

我以為她有聽到我說的話，因為她瞧了我好一會兒，接著，她便消失了。我在陽光下，獨自站在那裡，我知道我得留在碧廬。

當天下午，就在下午茶時間之前，我去葛洛斯太太的房間找她。

「今天上午發生了什麼事？你怎麼沒到教堂來？」她問。

「我回來跟傑索小姐談！」

葛洛斯太太克制住自己的驚訝。

「跟她談？你是說，她跟你說話了？」

「嗯，是的。」我說。

「她說了什麼？」

「她說她很痛苦……」我停了下來，幾乎不敢說出那個字，「受著地獄的苦！」

P. 62

葛洛斯太太驚駭地看著我。

我繼續往下說：「她想讓芙蘿拉也受這種苦！但是你不必擔心，」我很快地說出：「我決定寫信給孩子們的伯父。」

「噢，太好了，小姐，請寫信給他！」管家說道，幾乎快哭了出來。

「邁爾斯以為我不敢寫信給他的伯父，但是他錯了。他的伯父現在一定要知道這一切事情，他一定要知道我為什麼沒替孩子找別的學校。我會給他看校長寫的信。我會跟他說，我不能夠替這樣的孩子另外找學校，他之所以被開除，是因為……」

「我們也不知道原因啊，小姐。」葛洛斯太太說。

「……是因為他太邪惡了！只有這個原因，葛洛斯太太！當然，這都得怪他的伯父，留下孩子，讓他們跟那些可怕的人在一起，這完全是錯誤的。」

葛洛斯太太開始哭了起來。她不願相信邁爾斯是個壞孩子。

「我今天晚上就會動手寫信。」我說。

等孩子們上床睡覺後，我開始提筆寫信。窗外下著傾盆大雨，狂風吹得窗戶嘎吱作響。我望著芙蘿拉，她睡得很安詳。我拿起蠟燭，走到邁爾斯的房間，他還醒著。

「你怎麼還不睡？」我問。

P. 63

「我躺在這裡想事情。」他回答。

「你在想什麼事情？」

「我在想你，想我在這裡的生活，想你是如何照顧我的，還有想其他的所有一切。」他回答。

「你這話是什麼意思？」我焦急問。

「你知道的！你知道的！」他帶著笑容說道。

我們默默看著對方一會兒。

接著，我開口說：「你一定可以回到學校的，邁爾斯。不過不是回到之前的學校，我們會幫你找一間更好的學校。你待在家裡不快樂嗎？」

「噢，很快樂，但是我想要離開家，我是一個男孩，我要過一個男孩該有的生活。」他說。

我沒有作聲。男孩該有的生活是什麼？我感覺到邁爾斯所知道的事，遠比我還要多。

邁爾斯

• 邁爾斯要的是什麼？為什麼？
• 家庭教師為什麼不幫他另外找一間學校？
• 你想，邁爾斯還會回到學校嗎？

P. 64

「我的伯父一定要來碧廬一趟，他一定要做個決定，看要怎麼做才是。」他盯著天花板說。

「我已經在寫信給他。」我說。

「那就快把信寫完！」

我緩緩站起身，但並沒有離開房間，我沒辦法走出去。

「你回到碧廬之前，發生了什麼事，邁爾斯？還有，在你離家之前，又發生了什麼事？」我問。

他看著我，沒有回答我的問題。

「親愛的小邁爾斯！」我一邊說，一邊用雙手抱住他：「我只是想要幫助你，我只想要你也幫我，讓我來救你。」

這時，一道冷風吹拂過房間。邁爾斯突然大聲尖叫，我跳了起來。突然間，我發現自己站立在一片漆黑之中。

「噢，蠟燭被吹熄了！」我喊道。

「不，」邁爾斯說：「是我吹熄蠟燭的！」

第七章　離開

P.65

隔天，孩子們比起平時更加用功念書。邁爾斯對我尤其和善。午餐過後，他問我，要不要聽他彈奏一曲鋼琴。也許他是對於自己前一天的行為感到抱歉。我們一起步入教室，他開始彈奏樂曲。我不認為自己睡著了，但是有半個鐘頭之久，我完全忘記了芙蘿拉。當我再想到她的時候，我立刻跳了起來，環顧四周。

「芙蘿拉呢？」我問邁爾斯。

他笑著說：「我不知道！」他說完後，繼續彈著鋼琴。

「她一定是跟葛洛斯太太在一起。」我心想。我很快走下樓，去她的房間找她，但是沒有找著。

我和管家在房子裡找遍了，都沒有看到她的蹤影。

「她出去了，一定是跟她在一起！」我說。

「邁爾斯人呢？」葛洛斯太太問。

「他在樓上的教室裡，而且他的計畫得逞了！芙蘿拉跟傑索小姐碰面時，他想辦法讓我不會有動靜。現在，他也趁著這個空檔，可以去找昆特了。不過，我不介意。」我回答。

P.66

葛洛斯太太驚訝地望著我，焦急地問：「你寫信了嗎？」

我從口袋裡掏出信來，放在大廳的桌前。

「信寫好了，路克可以把信拿去寄。」我說。

路克是一名僕人。接著，我打開門，走了出去。

「你不穿上一件外套嗎？」葛洛斯太太問。

「沒時間了。」

我跑過草坪，前往芙蘿拉最喜歡的花園角落——那座湖。葛洛斯太太跟了上來。

「她應該在我見到傑索小姐出現的地

方，我一直懷疑她想要單獨回去那個地方。現在，她的哥哥替她安排了這件事。」我對管家說。

然而，那個地方一個人影也沒有。

我尋找小船，孩子們有時會搭這條小船遊湖。

「小船不見了！她搭小船去對岸了！」我驚呼道。

「她一個人嗎？但她還是小孩子！」葛洛斯太太回答。

「她不是一個人，而且當她跟傑索小姐在一起的時候，她就不是小孩子，而是一個年長的女人。走吧！我們沿著湖邊，去尋找她的下落。」我說。

不久，我們就找到了小船，小船被藏在蘆葦叢裡。不過我們並沒有看到芙蘿拉的蹤影。我們又走了一些距離，最後也看到了她的蹤影，她在田野裡。

P. 67

「她在那裡！」我們異口同聲地喊道。

芙蘿拉聽到我們的聲音，便露出了笑容。我們立刻衝到她的身邊，葛洛斯太太屈膝跪在地上，抱住孩子。

芙蘿拉先開口說話，她問道：「你的帽子和外套呢？邁爾斯人呢？」

「我會告訴你邁爾斯人在哪裡，如果你跟我說……」我聽見我自己這樣說到。

「說什麼？」

葛洛斯太太看著我，嚇得倒抽一口氣。但是她現在阻止不了我了。

「……親愛的，傑索小姐在哪裡呢？」

這時，我看見她了。她正站在湖的另一邊，盯著我們看。

「她在那裡！她在那裡！」我一邊喊叫，一邊用手指著那個方向。

我很確定葛洛斯太太和芙蘿拉也見到她了，但是芙蘿拉並沒有朝我指的方向望過去，她一臉嚴肅的小臉蛋，反倒是盯著我看。這嚇到我了。

「她就在那裡，你這個可憐的孩子，她在那裡，在那裡！你可以清楚地看到她，就像你可以清楚地看到我一樣！」我大聲咆哮道。

「小姐，你究竟看到了什麼？」葛洛斯太太說。

我可以從她臉上的表情看出來，她並不相信我。「你看不見她嗎？」我抓住她的手臂，大聲喊道：「快看啊，親愛的管家，快看！」

P. 68

「小姐，我什麼都沒看到啊。」她淡淡地回答。

接著，她雙手緊緊抱住小女孩。「那裡沒有人呀，親愛的。」她的聲音變得和善，「可憐的傑索小姐已經死了，怎麼還會出現在那裡？走吧！我們現在回家去！」

P. 70

芙蘿拉依舊盯著我看，她臉上的表情宛如一張面具，看起來既冷酷又醜陋。

「我沒有看到任何人、任何東西，我從沒看過什麼東西。」她朝著我大聲咆哮說：「我覺得你很殘酷，我不喜歡你！」

接著，她把臉埋進葛洛斯太太的衣服裡，大聲哭喊道：「帶我走！拜託！帶我遠離她！」

我為這個孩子感到難過，我無法再為她做什麼了。

「我已經盡了最大的努力來挽救你，但是，我失去你了。葛洛斯太太，帶她回屋子裡吧！」我說。

芙蘿拉

- 這個時候，芙蘿拉的感受如何？
- 她對家庭教師的看法是什麼？
- 如今，芙蘿拉會發生什麼事？

事發之後，我不太記得後來的事了。我想，我大概躺在草地上哭泣。我抬頭望著天空，天色一片漆黑，而我的臉都濕了。我走回屋裡，逕自回房，房間裡已經看不到芙蘿拉的床了。

隔天，葛洛斯太太一個大早就帶來一些壞消息。

P. 71

「小姐，芙蘿拉病了，她哭了一整夜。她很怕你！」

「她有提到傑索小姐嗎？」

「沒有，小姐。她說她沒看到湖那裡有任何人。」

「孩子生來就聰明，而昆特和傑索小姐讓他們更精明了。現在，芙蘿拉向她的伯父抱怨我，因為她想要擺脫我。」

「她不想要再見到你了，小姐。」

「你來，是要我離開碧廬嗎？」我問。接著，不等她回答，我說：「我有一個更好的主意，你一定要離開碧廬，葛洛斯太太。帶著芙蘿拉，去倫敦找她的伯父。我和邁爾斯留在這裡。我很確信他有事情要告訴我，只是需要多一點時間。請你盡快離開吧。」

葛洛斯太太露出有些困窘的表情，但是沒有多說什麼。

「但你可能不想要離開。」我說。

「我會離開。」她一邊說，一邊把手放在我的手上，「我今天早上就走。你說得對，小姐，我不能夠留在這裡。」

這時她突然哭了出來。

「她說了一些很可怕的事情……」她啜泣道。

「和我有關？」

「是的，小姐。」她擦乾眼淚說：「她
說的那番話，真的很嚇人，不知道她是
從哪裡學來的。」她看看她的錶，說道：
「我現在得回去她身邊照顧她。」

P.72

「記住！我們的雇主現在應該已經收到
我的信了，所以他應該已經知道邁爾斯
的事。」我說。

「你的信並沒有寄出去，小姐。邁爾斯
主人……」

「……他把信拿走了？」我倒抽了一口
氣。

她說：「路克沒有把信寄出去，可是當
我和芙蘿拉回來的時候，就沒有看到桌
上有信了。」她又開始哭泣起來，「他在
學校可能也是會做這種事，小姐！」她啜
泣著說，「信可能是被他偷走的！」

「嗯，我在信中所提到的事，都是他已
經知道的事。別擔心，葛洛斯太太，他
會跟我說明一切的。現在，快走吧！」我
回答。

第八章　永遠失去

P.73

之後，當我來到樓下，屋子裡空蕩蕩
的，很安靜。我感覺到焦慮和孤寂。僕
人們看著我，但是沒有多問管家突然離
開的事。

這一整天，我都沒有看到邁爾斯。一
直到晚餐時間，他才出現。當時我已經
坐在餐廳裡，晚餐也都上桌了。他站在
我身旁，兩隻手插進口袋裡。

「芙蘿拉病得很重嗎？」他問。

「芙蘿拉？不，她病得不重。她待在倫
敦，很快就會復原，對她來說，碧廬這
個地方不太好。過來，坐這裡，這裡有
要給你的一些肉。」

他拿起餐盤坐下，我們靜靜地吃著晚
餐。

用過晚餐後，我請女僕將桌上收拾乾
淨。當女僕在收拾晚餐時，邁爾斯站起
身，望向窗外。等到女僕離開餐室後，
他轉過身來望著我，說道：「好啦！我們
現在獨處了！」

「算是吧。」我擠出笑容。

他走過來，站在我面前。

「沒錯。」他說：「當然，還有其他人在
這裡，但是他們並不重要，不是嗎？」

P.75

「那要視情況而定。」

117

「沒錯，凡事都得視情況而定！」他說。

他走回窗戶邊，把頭靠在窗戶的玻璃上。他顯得不太自在，有些焦慮。他是在找他看不見的東西嗎？

最後，他轉過身來說：「嗯，我很高興碧廬對我來說沒有什麼不好！」

「你今天玩得開心嗎？」

「噢，開心。我走了好幾英里，沒有這麼自由過。」

「你喜歡這樣嗎？」

他笑了笑，然後說：「那你喜歡嗎？」在我還沒來得及回答之前，他繼續往下說：「你待在這裡，比我還要孤單。你介意嗎？」

「留在這裡照顧你嗎？不，當然不介意，所以我才留在這裡呀。」

「你留下來，就只是為了我？」

「當然，我是你的朋友。你還記得那個暴風夜嗎？我告訴過你，我只想要幫助你。」

他神經緊繃地笑道：「是啊，記得。不過，那只是因為你要我替你做件事情。」他補充說。

「沒錯。你還記得是什麼事嗎？」

「噢，記得，你要我告訴你一件事。」他開心說。

P. 76

「沒錯。」

「這就是你留在這裡的原因嗎？」

「嗯，是的，沒錯。」

他沉默良久，最後開口說：「我一定要我此時此刻就告訴你嗎？」

「沒錯。」

突然，我感覺到他有一點怕我。

「你想再出門一次嗎？」我輕聲地問。

「很想。」他對著我笑了笑。

我等候著他開口。

「好吧，我會把一切事情都告訴你，但不是現在。」他說。

「為什麼現在不可以？」

「我得去找路克。」

這是謊言。是我讓他撒了謊，我自己覺得過不去，也為他感到難過。

謊言

• 家庭教師究竟想知道什麼？
• 邁爾斯為什麼要對她撒謊？
• 家庭教師為什麼為他感到難過？

P. 77

「好吧，你去找路克，我等你。但是，在你離開之前，告訴我一件事，你昨天下午有拿走我的信嗎？」我說。

就在這時候，邁爾斯身後的窗戶，突然出現彼得·昆特的臉！我立刻抓住男孩，把他拉向我，我不想讓他看到窗外那個惡人。這一刻，我可以強烈感受到，我和昆特悄然無聲地在爭奪著孩子的靈魂。

「是的，是我拿的。」邁爾斯壓低嗓音說，他的小臉蛋跟窗戶上的那張臉一樣蒼白。

我雙手抱住他，讓他靠向我。他的身體發燙，我可以感覺到他的心跳。

「你為什麼把信拿走？」我說。

「想看你在信中說了我什麼。」

「你看了信了？」

「看了。」他低聲地說道。

我抬起頭，以為會在窗戶那裡看到昆特的臉，但是他不在了。邁爾斯得救了！

「結果你卻什麼也沒看到！」我開心得幾乎是用喊的。

「什麼也沒有，所以我把信給燒掉了。」

「邁爾斯，你在學校的時候，也會拿走信或其他東西嗎？所以你才不能回學校？」

「你知道我不能回學校的事？」他問。

P. 79

「我什麼都知道。」

「什麼都知道？」

「什麼都知道，所以你到底有沒有……？」我說不出那個字。

「有沒有偷東西？沒有！」

「那麼，你做了什麼事？」

他深呼吸兩三次，「嗯，我透露了事情。」

「你是跟誰透露的？」

他一臉困惑，「我不知道！我不記得他們的名字了。」

「你是跟很多人透露嗎？」

「不，我只跟我喜歡的人講，然後他們再跟其他人說。」

他又深呼吸了一下，額頭佈滿了汗珠。

「然後這些人再去跟校長講。」

「對。我很驚訝，校長把他們的事告訴了你。」他說。

「他並沒有說。那是什麼事呢，邁爾斯？」

他轉過身，望向窗戶。就在這時，昆特那張蒼白的臉又再度出現。我一陣不安，又抓住麥爾斯，把他抱住。

「沒事了，沒事了！」我尖聲呼喊。

「她在這裡嗎？」邁爾斯倒抽一口氣，「傑索小姐？」

「那不是傑索小姐。你看，那裡！」我呼喊道。

邁爾斯感到困惑，他的目光搜尋著房間內那張他看不見的臉。

P. 80

「那麼是他嗎？」他生氣地大喊。

「誰？」

「彼得·昆特，你這個惡魔！你在哪裡？」

「這一切現在都不重要了，邁爾斯，我現在救出你了，他永遠失去你了。看！他在那裡！」我說。

邁爾斯很快地轉身望向窗外，他只看見窗外寂靜的白晝。接著，他發出痛苦的叫聲，然後往後倒。我抓住他，把他抱住。

最後一刻，我才發現，他的小心臟不再跳動了。

119

ANSWER KEY

Before Reading

Pages 8-9

1 a) 5   b) 3   c) 2, 6   d) 1, 4
3 a) T   b) F

Pages 10-11

4 a) 2   b) 1   c) 4   d) 3
5 a) headmaster
  b) maid
  c) housekeeper
  d) governess
6 Mrs. Grose and the governess.
7 a) 4   b) 3   c) 1   d) 2

Pages 12-13

8 b, c, e
9 a
10 a) 5   b) 3   c) 7   d) 2

Page 19

• He's young, handsome and well-dressed. He's also rich and charming.
• No, he isn't.
• Yes, she does.
• Yes, he is.

Page 26

• *boarding*: a school where students live for part of the year
• *mixed:* a school for both boys and girls
• *nursery*: a school for children between 3 and 5 years old
• *public*: an expensive private school
• *secondary*: a school for children between 11 and 16 or 18 years old
• *comprehensive*: a secondary school offering the curricula of a grammar school, a technical school, and a secondary modern school, with no division into separate compartments

After Reading

- She thinks that the children can see the ghosts.
- Flora didn't say anything to her about the ghost.
- Yes, she probably does.

- He wants to play with other boys. Perhaps he's bored at home.
- She doesn't want to speak to his uncle about it.

- She felt afraid and angry.
- Flora hated her because she thought she was cruel.

- She wants to know what happened before Miles went away to school and what happened at school.
- He doesn't want to tell her the truth. Perhaps he's embarrassed.
- Because he she has made him tell a lie and Miles is usually a good boy.

4 a) 2   b) 2   c) 3   d) 1   e) 1
   f) 3   g) 2   h) 3   i) 1   j) 3

5 a) Mrs. Grose
   b) the master
   c) the master and Peter Quint
   d) Miles
   e) Miss Jessel

6
- Three.
- The narrator (perhaps Henry James himself); Douglas; the governess.
- The narrator and Douglas are friends. They are spending Christmas in an old house with other friends. Douglas met the governess when he was young. She gave him the manuscript of her story. The governess's story is inside Douglas's story, and his story is inside the narrator's story.

7
- Because she respects her. A governess is more important than a housekeeper.

8
- Because she wants to forget the problem.

9
- A: She'll recognize her. She'll be able to tell me who she is.
- B: The headmaster's letter is very silly! Have you ever met a sweeter child than Miles?
- C: Those children aren't like ordinary children. They're too beautiful and too good.

10 a) romantic
b) charming, friendly
c) friendly, kind
d) charming, clever
e) sad
f) dishonest

11
a) The master of Bly to the governess when they met in London.
b) The governess to Mrs. Grose after the governess read the headmaster's letter to Mrs. Grose.
c) Mrs. Grose to the governess after the governess saw Quint at the window.
d) The governess to Mrs. Grose after the governess saw Miss Jessel at the lake.
e) Flora to the governess when the governess left the bedroom one night.
f) Miles to the governess after Mrs. Grose and Flora left.

12
a) In the country.
b) He was a priest.
c) She needed to work.
d) He was young, handsome and well-dressed.
e) Perhaps she was in love with him.
f) She wanted to show him that she could do the job well.
g) She was young and pretty.
h) Perhaps.

14
a) They didn't behave well. They weren't responsible people. They didn't have much respect for others.
b) Perhaps she imagines that Miss Jessel killed herself because she was expecting Quint's baby.

15
• She listens to the governess and believes her. She also gives the governess information about Quint and Miss Jessel.

16 a) 2 b) 2 c) 1 d) 1
e) 1 f) 2 g) 2 h) 1

17
a) She imagined them.
b) Because they didn't behave well.
c) Because she wanted to show him that she could do the job without his help.
d) Perhaps she was very frightened.
e) She left Bly and found another job.

18 a) 3 b) 1 c) 4 d) 2

20
a) thought
b) saw
c) was going
d) was staring

21
a) was
b) gasped
c) stared
d) was looking for

22
a) seen
b) recognize
c) doing
d) look

23 1. b   2. d   3. c   4. a

24
a) were sent
b) younger than
c) difficult
d) have many

25
a) responsible
b) triumphant
c) innocent
d) cruel
e) wicked

26
a) behavior
b) decision
c) disappointment
d) excitement
e) imagination
f) suspicion

Test

Pages 90-91

1 a) 2   b) 1   c) 2   d) 2
2 a) 3   b) 4   c) 1   d) 2   e) 3

國家圖書館出版品預行編目資料

碧廬冤孽 / Henry James 著；Jennifer
Gascoigne 改寫；盧相如 譯. 一初版. 一[臺北市]
：寂天文化, 2017.10 面；公分. 中英對照; 譯自：
The Turn of the Screw

ISBN 978-986-318-613-7 (平裝附光碟片)

874.57   106016438

原著 _ Henry James

改寫 _ Jennifer Gascoigne

譯者 _ 盧相如

校對 _ 陳慧莉

編輯 _ 安卡斯

製程管理 _ 洪巧玲

出版者 _ 寂天文化事業股份有限公司

電話 _ +886-2-2365-9739

傳真 _ +886-2-2365-9835

網址 _ www.icosmos.com.tw

讀者服務 _ onlineservice@icosmos.com.tw

出版日期 _ 2017年10月 初版一刷（250101）

郵撥帳號 _ 1998620-0 寂天文化事業股份有限公司